Dradin, In Love

A Tale of Elsewhen & Otherwhere

Jeff VanderMeer

Illustrations by Michael Shores

Buzzcity Press
Tallahassee, Florida

BUZZCITY PRESS
P.O. Box 38190
Tallahassee, FL 32315 U.S.A.
annk@freenet.scri.fsu.edu

Buzzcity First Editions
Series Editor: Ann Kennedy
Cover design consultant: Duane Bray

Printer: BookMasters
2541 Ashland Road,
P.O. Box 2139,
Mansfield, OH 44905
Telephone number: 1-800-537-6727.

Special thanks to: Cindy Matthews, Keith Bender, and the fine staff at BookMasters; Paula held; Jennifer Shettle; Duane Bray; the Florida Dept. of State, Division of Cultural Affairs; the Leon Station branch of the Tallahassee Post Office; Sean Winans & Municipal Code Corporation.

Text Copyright 1996 Jeff VanderMeer
Illustrations Copyright 1996 Michael Shores

All rights reserved. No portion of this book may be reprinted without express written consent of the publisher, save for short excerpts for review purposes.

Please send S.A.S.E. to Buzzcity Press for information about future Buzzcity First Editions as well as *The Silver Web*, a magazine of the surreal, which serves as Buzzcity Press' flagship publication. *Dradin, In Love* is available for $11.50 postpaid directly from the publisher ($13.50 postpaid for foreign orders)

ISBN O-9652200-0-1

"What can be said about Ambergris that has not already been said? Every minute section of the city, no matter how seemingly superfluous, has a complex, even devious, part to play in the communal life. And no matter how often I stroll down Albumuth Boulevard, I never lose my sense of the city's incomparable splendor — its love of ritual, its passion for music, its infinite capacity for the beautiful cruelty."
— Voss Bender, *Memoirs of a Composer,* Vol. No. I, page 558, Ministry of Whimsy Press

Nothing in her spoke of the rough rude world surrounding Dradin, nor of the great, unmapped southern jungles from which he had just returned

I.

DRADIN, IN LOVE, beneath the window of his love, staring up at her while crowds surge and seethe around him, bumping and bruising him all unawares in their rough-clothed, bright-rouged thousands. For Dradin watches *her*, she taking dictation from a machine, an inscrutable block of gray from which sprout the earphones she wears over her oval, egg-shaped, delicate head. Dradin is struck dumb and dumber still by the seraphim blue of her eyes and the cascade of long and lustrous black hair over her shoulders, her pale face gloomy against the glass and masked by the reflection of the graying sky above. She is three stories up, ensconced in brick and mortar, almost a monument, her seat near the window just above the sign that reads "Hoegbotton & Sons, Distributors." Hoegbotton & Sons: the largest importer and exporter in all of lawless Ambergris, that oldest of cities named for the most valuable and secret part of the whale. Hoegbotton & Sons: boxes and boxes of depravities shipped for the amusement of the decadent from far, far Surphasia and the nether regions of the Occident, those places that moisten, ripen, and decay in a blink. And yet, Dradin surmises, she looks as if she comes from more contented stock, not a stay-at-home, but uncomfortable abroad, unless traveling on the arm of her lover. Does she have a lover? A husband? Are her parents yet living? Does she like the opera or the bawdy theatre shows put on down by the docks, where the creaking limbs of laborers load the crates of Hoegbotton & Sons onto barges that take the measure of the mighty River Moth as it flows, sludge-filled and torpid, down into the rapid swell of the sea? If she likes the theatre, I can at least afford her, Dradin thinks, gawping up at her. His long hair slides down into his face, but so struck is he that he does not care. The heat withers him this far from the river, but he ignores the noose of sweat round his neck.

Dradin, dressed in black with dusty white collar, dusty black shoes, and the demeanor of an out-of-work missionary (which indeed he is), had not meant to see the woman. Dradin had not meant to look up at all. He had been looking *down* to pick up the coins he had lost through a hole in his threadbare trousers, their seat torn by the lurching carriage ride from the docks into Ambergris, the carriage drawn by a horse bound for the glue factory, perhaps taken to the slaughter yards that very day — the day before the Festival of the Freshwater Squid as the carriage driver took pains to inform him, perhaps hoping Dradin would require his further services. But it was all Dradin could do to stay seated as they made their way to a hostel, deposited his baggage in a room, and returned once more to the merchant districts — to catch a bit of local color, a bite to eat — where he and the carriage driver parted company. The driver's mangy beast had left its stale smell on Dradin, but it was a necessary beast nonetheless, for he could never have afforded a mechanized horse, a vehicle of smoke and oil. Not when he would soon be down to his last coins and in desperate need of a job, the job he had come to Ambergris to find, for his former teacher at the Morrow Religious Academy — a certain Cadimon Signal — preached from Ambergris' religious quarter, and surely, what with the festivities, there would be work?

Dradin, In Love

But when Dradin picked up his coins, he regained his feet rather too jauntily, spun and rattled by a ragtag gang of jackanapes who ran past him, and his gaze had come up on the gray, rain-threatening sky, and swung through to the window he now watched with such intensity.

The woman had long, delicate fingers that typed to their own peculiar rhythms, so that she might as well have been playing Voss Bender's Fifth, diving to the desperate lows and soaring to the magnificent highs that Voss Bender claimed as his territory. When her face became, for the moment, revealed to Dradin through the glare of glass — a slight forward motion to advance the tape, perhaps, or a hand run through her hair — he could see that her features, a match for her hands, were reserved, streamlined, artful. Nothing in her spoke of the rough rude world surrounding Dradin, nor of the great, unmapped southern jungles from which he had just returned; where the black panther and the blacker mamba waited with such malign intent; where he had been so consumed by fever and by doubt and by lack of converts to his religion that he had come back into the charted territory of laws and governments, where, sweet joy, there existed women like the creature in the window above him. Watching her, his blood simmering within him, Dradin wondered if he was dreaming her, she a haloed, burning vision of salvation, soon to disappear mirage-like, so that he might once more be cocooned within his fever, in the jungle, in the darkness.

But it was not a dream and, of a sudden, Dradin broke from his reverie, knowing she might see him, so vulnerable, or that passersby might guess at his intent and reveal it to her before he was ready. For the real world surrounded him, from the stink of vegetables in the drains to the *sweet* of half-gnawed hamhocks in the trash; the clip-clop-stomp of horse and the rattled honk of motored vehicles; the rustle-whisper of mushroom dwellers disturbed from daily slumber and, from somewhere hidden, the sound of a baroque and lilting music, crackly as if played on a phonograph. People knocked into him, allowed him no space to move: merchants and jugglers and knife salesmen and sidewalk barbers and tourists and prostitutes and sailors on leave from their ships; even the odd pale-faced young tough, smiling a gangrenous smile.

Dradin realized he must act, and yet he was too shy to approach her, to fling open the door to Hoegbotton & Sons, dash up the three flights of stairs and, unannounced (and perhaps unwanted) and unwashed, come before her dusty and smitten, a twelve o'clock shadow upon his chin. Obvious that he had come from the Great Beyond, for he still stank of the jungle rot and jungle excess. No, no. He must not thrust himself upon her.

But what, then, to do? Dradin's thoughts tumbled one over the other like distraught clowns and he was close to panic, close to wringing his hands in the way his mother had disapproved of but that indicated nothing unusual in a missionary, when a thought came to him and left him speechless at his own ingenuity.

A bauble, of course. A present. A trifle, at his expense, to show his love for her. Dradin looked up and down the street, behind and below him for a shop that might hold a treasure to touch, intrigue, and, ultimately, keep her. Madame Lowery's Crochets? The Lady's Emporium? Jessible's Jewelry Store? No, no, no. For what if she were a Modern, a woman who would not be kept or kept pregnant, but moved in the same circles as the artisans and writers, the actors and singers? What an insult such a gift would be to her then. What an insensitive man she would think him to be, and what an insensitive man he *would* be. Had all his months in the jungle peeled away his common sense, layer by layer, until he was as naked as an orangutan? No, it would not do. He could not buy clothing, chocolates, nor even flowers, for these gifts were too forward, unsubtle, uncouth, and lacking in imagination. Besides, they —

— and his roving gaze, touching on the ruined aqueduct

that divided the two sides of the street like the giant fossilized spine of a long, lean shark, locked in on the distant opposite shore and the modern sign with the double curlicues and the bold lines of type that proclaimed *Borges Bookstore*, and right there, on Albumuth Boulevard, the filthiest, most sublime, and richest thoroughfare in all of Ambergris, Dradin realized he had found the perfect gift. Nothing could be better than a book, or more mysterious, and nothing could draw her more perfectly to him.

Still dusty and alone in the swirl of the city — a voyeur amongst her skirts — Dradin set out toward the opposite side, threading himself between street players and pimps, card sharks and candy sellers, through the aqueduct, and, braving the snarl of twin stone lions atop a final archway, came at last to *Borges Bookstore*. It had splendid antique windows, gilt embroidered, with letters that read:

GIFTS FOR ANY OCCASION:

* THE HISTORY OF THE RIVER MOTH *
* GAMBLING PRACTICES OF THE OUTLANDS *
* THE RELIGIOUS QUARTER ON 15 Ls. A DAY *
* SQUID POACHING ON THE HIGH SEAS *
* CORRUPTION IN THE MERCHANT DISTRICT *
* ARCHITECTURE OF ALBUMUTH BOULEVARD *
ALSO, *The Hoegbotton Series of Guidebooks & Maps to the Festival, Safe Places, Hazards, and Blindfolds.*

Book upon piled book mentioned in the silvery scrawl, and beyond the glass the quiet, slow movements of bibliophiles, feasting upon the genuine articles. It made Dradin forget to breathe, and not simply because this place would have a gift for his dearest, his most beloved, the woman in the window, but because he had been away from the world for a year and, now back, he found the accoutrements of civilization comforted him. His father, that tortured soul, was still a great reader, between the bouts of drinking, despite the erosion of encroaching years, and Dradin could remember many a time that the man had, honking his red, red nose — a monstrosity of a nose, out of proportion to anything in the family line — read and wept at the sangfroid exploits of two poor debutantes named Juliette and Justine as they progressed from poverty to prostitution, to the jungles and back again, weepy with joy as they rediscovered wealth and went on to have wonderful adventures up and down the length and breadth of the River Moth, until finally pristine Justine expired from the pressure of tragedies wreaked upon her.

It made Dradin swell with pride to think that the woman at the window was more beautiful than either Juliette or Justine, far more beautiful, and likely more stalwart besides. (And yet, Dradin admitted, in the delicacy of her features, the pale gloss of her lips, he espied an innately breakable quality as well.)

Thus thinking, Dradin pushed open the glass door, the lacquered oak frame a-creak, and a bell chimed once, twice, thrice. On the thrice chime, a clerk dressed all in dark greens, sleeves spiked with gold cuff links, came forward, shoes soundless on the thick carpet, bowed, and asked, "How may I help you?"

To which Dradin explained that he sought a gift for a woman. "Not a woman I know," he said, "but a woman I should like to know."

The clerk, a rake of a lad with dirty brown hair and a face as subtle as mutton pie, winked wryly, smiled, and said, "I understand, sir, and I have *precisely* the book for you. It arrived a fortnight ago from the Ministry of Whimsy imprint — an Occidental publisher, sir. Please follow me."

The clerk led Dradin past mountainous shelves of history texts perused by shriveled prunes of men dressed in orange pantaloons — buffoons from university, no doubt, practicing for some baroque Voss Bender revival — and voluminous mantels of fictions and pastorals, neglected except by a widow in black and a child of twelve with thick, thick glasses, then

Dradin, In Love

exhaustive columns of philosophy on which the dust had settled thicker still, until finally they reached a corner hidden by "Funerals" entitled "Objects of Desire."

The clerk pulled out an elegant eight-by-eleven book lined with soft velvet and gold leaf. "It is called *The Refraction of Light in a Prison* and in it can be found the collected wisdom of the last remaining Truffidian monks, who have long been imprisoned in the dark towers of the Kalif. It was snuck out of those dark towers by an intrepid adventurer who — "

"Who was not a son of Hoegbotton, I hope," Dradin said, because it was well known that Hoegbotton & Sons dealt in all sorts of gimmickry and mimicry, and he did not like to think that he was giving his love an item she might have unpacked and catalogued herself.

"Hoegbotton & Sons? No, sir. Not a son of Hoegbotton. We do not deal with Hoegbotton & Sons (except inasmuch as we are contracted to carry their guidebooks) as their practices are . . . how shall I put it? . . . *questionable*. With neither Hoegbotton nor his sons do we deal. But where was I? The Truffidians.

"They are experts at the art of cataloguing passion, with this grave distinction: that when I say to you, sir, 'passion,' I mean the word in its most general sense, a sense that does not allow for intimacies of the kind that might strike the lady you *wish to know better* as too vulgar. It merely speaks to the general — the *incorporeal*, as one more highly witted than I might say. It shall not offend; rather, it shall lend to the gift-giver an aura of mystery that may prove permanently alluring."

The clerk proffered the book for inspection, but Dradin merely touched the svelte cover with his hand and said no, for he had had the most delightful thought: that he could explore those pages at the same time as his love. The thought made his hands tremble as they had not trembled since the fever ruled his body and he feared he might die. He imagined his hand atop hers as they turned the pages, her eyes caressing the same chapter and paragraph, the same line and word; thus could they learn of passion together but separate.

"Excellent, excellent," Dradin said, and, after a tic of hesitation — for he was much closer to penniless than penniful — he added, "but I shall need two," and then as the clerk's eyebrows rose like the startled silhouettes of twin sea gulls upon finding that a fish within their grasp is actually a snark, he stuttered, "A-a-and a map. A map of the city. For the festival."

"Of course," said the clerk, as if to say, *Converts all around, eh?*

Dradin, dour-faced, said only, "Wrap this one and I will take the other unwrapped, along with the map," and stood stiff, brimming over with urgency, as the clerk dawdled and digressed. He knew well the clerk's thoughts: *a rogue priest, ungodly and unbound by any covenant made with God.* And perhaps the clerk was right, but did not canonical law provide for the unforeseen and the estranged, for the combination of beauty and the bizarre of which the jungle was itself composed? How else could one encompass and explain the terrible grace of the Hull Peoples, who lived within the caves hewn by a waterfall, and who, when dispossessed by Dradin and sent to the missionary fort, complained of the silence, the silence of God, how God would not talk to them, for what else was the play of water upon the rocks but the voice of God? He had had to send them back to their waterfall, for he could not bear the haunted looks upon their faces, the disorientation blossoming in their eyes like a deadly and deadening flower.

Dradin had first taken a lover in the jungles: a sweaty woman priest whose kisses smothered and suffocated him even as they brought him back to the world of flesh. Had she infected his mission? No, for he had tried so very hard for conversions, despite their scarcity. Even confronted by savage beast, savage plant, and just plain savage he had persevered. Perhaps persevered for too long, in the face of too many obstacles, his hair proof of his tenacity — the stark black streaked with white or,

Dradin, In Love

in certain light, stark white shot through with black, each strand of white attributable to the jungle fever (so cold it burned, his skin glacial), each strand of black a testament to being alive afterwards.

Finally, the clerk tied a lime green bow around a bright red package: gaudy but serviceable. Dradin dropped the necessary coin on the marble counter, stuck the map in the unwrapped copy, and with a frown to the clerk, walked to the door.

Out in the gray glare of the street, the heat and the bustling confusion struck Dradin and he thought he was lost, lost in the jungles that he had only just fled, lost so he would never again find his lady. His breaths came ragged and he put a hand to his temple, for he felt faint yet giddy.

Gathering his strength, he plunged into the muddle of sweating flesh, sweating clothes, sweating cobblestones. He rushed past the twin lions, their asses waggling at him as if they knew very well what he was up to, the arches, and then a vanguard of mango sellers, followed by an army of elderly dowager women with brimming stomachs and deep-pouched aprons, determined to buy up every last fruit or legume; young pups in play nipped at his heels, and, lord help him, he was delivered pell-mell in a pile, delivered with a stumble and a bruise to the opposite sidewalk, there to stare up once again at his lady love. Could any passage be more perilous than that daylight passage across Albumuth Boulevard, unless it was to cross the Moth at flood time?

Undaunted, Dradin sprang to his feet, his two books secure, one under each arm, and smiled to himself.

The woman. She had not moved from her station on the third floor; Dradin could tell, for he stood exactly as he had previous, upon the same crack in the pavement, and she was exactly as before, down to the pattern of shadows across the glass. Her rigid bearing brought questions half-stumbling to his lips. Did they did not give her time for lunch? Did they make a virtue out of vice and virtually imprison her, enslave her to a cruel schedule? What had the clerk said? That Hoegbotton & Sons practices were *questionable*? He wanted to march into the building and talk to her superior, be her hero, but his dilemma was of a more practical kind: he did not wish to reveal himself as yet and thus needed a messenger for his gift.

Dradin searched the babble of people and his vision blurred, the world simplified to a sea of walking clothes: cufflinks and ragged trousers, blouses dancing with skirts, tall cotton hats and shoes with loose laces. How to distinguish? How to know whom to approach?

Fingers tugged at his shoulder and someone said, "Do you want to buy her?"

Buy her? Glancing down, Dradin found himself confronted by a singular man. This singular soul looked to be, it must be said, almost one muscle, a squat man with a low center of gravity, and yet perhaps the source of levity despite this: in short, a dwarf. How could one miss him? He wore a jacket and vest red as a freshly slaughtered carcass and claribel pleated trousers dark as crusted blood and shoes tipped with steel. A permanent grin molded the sides of his mouth so rigidly that, on second glance, Dradin wondered if it might not be a grimace. Melon bald, the dwarf was tattooed from head to foot.

The tattoo — which first appeared to be a birthmark or fungal growth — rendered Dradin speechless so that the dwarf said to him not once, but twice, "Are you all right, sir?"

While Dradin just stared, gap-jawed like a young jackdaw with naive fluff for wing feathers. For the dwarf had, tattooed from a point on the top of his head, and extending downward, a precise and detailed map of the River Moth, complete with the names of cities etched in black against the red dots that represented them. The river flowed a dark blue-green, thickening and thinning in places, dribbling up over the dwarf's left eyelid, skirting the midnight black of the eye itself, and down past taut lines of nose and mouth, curving over the generous chin and, like an exotic snake act, disappearing into the dwarf's vest and chest hair. A map of the lands beyond spread out from the River Moth. The northern cities of Dradin's youth — Belezar, Stockton, and Morrow (the last where his father still lived) — were clustered upon the dwarf's brow and there, upon the lower neck, almost the back, if one were to niggle, lay the jungles of Dradin's last year: a solid wall of green drawn with a jeweler's precision, the only hint of civilization a few smudges of red that denoted church enclaves. Dradin could have traced the line that marked his own dismal travels. He grinned, and he had to stop himself from putting out a hand to touch the dwarf's head for it had occurred to him that the dwarf's body served as a time line. Did it not show Dradin's birthplace and early years in the north as well as his slow descent into the south, the jungles, and now, more southern still, Ambergris? Could he not, if he were to see the entire tattoo, trace his descent further south, to the seas into which flowed the River Moth? Could he not chart his future, as it were? He would have laughed if not aware of the impropriety of doing so.

"Incredible," Dradin said.

"Incredible," echoed the dwarf, and smiled, revealing large yellowed teeth scattered between the gaping black of absent incisors and molars. "My father Alberich did it for me when I stopped growing. I was to be part of his show — he was a river boat pilot for tourists — and thus he traced upon my skin the course he plotted for them. It hurt like a thousand devils curling hooks into my flesh, but now I am, indeed, incredible. Do you wish to buy her? My name is Dvorak Nibelung." From within this storm of information, the dwarf extended a blunt, whorled hand that, when Dradin took it, was cool to the touch, and very rough.

"My name is Dradin."

"Dradin," Dvorak said. "Dradin. I say again, do you wish to buy her?"

"Buy who?"

"The woman in the window."

Dradin frowned. "No, of course I don't wish to buy her."

Dvorak looked up at him with black, watery eyes. Dradin could smell the strong musk of river water and silt on the dwarf, mixed with the sharp tang of an addictive, *ghittlnut*.

Dvorak said, "Must I tell you that she is only an image in a window? She is no more real to you. Seeing her, you fall in love. But: if you desire, I can I find you a woman who looks like her. She will do anything for money. Would you like such a woman?"

"No," Dradin said, and would have turned away if there had been room in the swirl of people to do so without appearing rude. Dvorak's hand found his arm again.

"If you do not wish to buy her, what do you wish to do with her?" Dvorak's voice was flat with miscomprehension.

"I wish to . . . I wish to woo her. I need to give her this book." And, then, if only to be rid of him, Dradin said, "Would you take this book to her and say that it comes from an admirer who wishes her to read it?"

To Dradin's surprise, Dvorak began to make huffing sounds, soft but then louder, until the River Moth changed course across the whorls of his face and something fastened to the inside of his jacket clicked together with a hundred deadly shivers.

Dradin's face turned scarlet.

"I suppose I will have to find someone else."

He took from his pocket two burnished gold coins engraved with the face of Trillian, the Great Banker, dead these forty years, and prepared to turn sharply on his heel.

Dvorak sobered and tugged yet a third time on his arm. "No, no, sir. Forgive me. Forgive me if I've offended, if I've made you angry," and the hand pulled at the gift-wrapped book in the crook of Dradin's shoulder. "I will take the book to the woman in the window. It is no great chore, for I already trade with Hoegbotton & Sons, see," and he pulled open the left side of his jacket to reveal five rows of cutlery: serrated and double-

Dradin, In Love

edged, made of whale bone and of steel, hilted in engraved wood and thick leather. "See," he said again. "I peddle knives for them outside their offices. I know this building," and he pointed at the solid brick. "Please?"

Dradin, painfully aware of the dwarf's claustrophobic closeness, the reek of him, would have said no, would have turned and said not only no, but *How dare you touch a man of God?*, but then what? He must make acquaintance with one or another of these people, pull some ruffian off the dusty sidewalk, for he could not do the deed himself. He knew this in the way his knees shook the closer he came to Hoegbotton & Sons, the way his words rattled around his mouth, came out mumbled and masticated into disconnected syllables.

Dradin shook Dvorak's hand off the book. "Yes, yes, you may give her the book." He placed the book in Dvorak's arms. "But hurry about it." A sense of relief lifted the weight of heat from his shoulders. He dropped the coins into a pocket of Dvorak's jacket. "Go on," and he waved a hand.

"Thank you, sir," Dvorak said. "But, should you not meet with me again, tomorrow, at the same hour, so you may know her thoughts? So you may gift her a second time, should you desire?"

"Shouldn't I wait to see her now?"

Dvorak shook his head. "No. Where is the mystery, the romance? Trust me: better that you disappear into the crowds. Better indeed. Then she will wonder at your appearance, your bearing, and have only the riddle of the gift to guide her. You see?"

"No, I don't. I don't see at all. I must be confident. I must allow her to — "

"You are right — you do not see at all. Sir, are you or are you not a priest?"

"Yes, but — "

"You do not think it best to delay her knowing of this until the right moment? You do not think she will find it odd a priest should woo her? Sir, you wear the clothes of a missionary, but she is no ordinary convert."

And now Dradin did see. And wondered why he had not seen before. He must lead her gently into the particulars of his occupation. He must not boldly announce it for fear of scaring her off.

"You are right," Dradin said. "You are right, of course."

Dvorak patted his arm. "Trust me, sir."

"Tomorrow then."

"Tomorrow, and bring more coin, for I cannot live on good will alone."

"Of course," Dradin said.

Dvorak bowed, turned, walked up to the door of Hoegbotton & Sons, and — quick and smooth and graceful — disappeared inside.

Dradin looked up at his love, wondering if he had made a mistake. Her lips still called to him and the entire sky seemed concentrated in her eyes, but he followed the dwarf's advice and, lighthearted, disappeared into the crowds.

Did they dream of giant mushrooms, gray caps agleam with the dark light of a midnight sun? Did they dream of a world lit only by the phosphorescent splendor of their charges?

II.

DRADIN, HAPPIER THAN he had been since dropping the fever at the Sisters of Mercy Hospital, some five hundred miles away and three months in the past, sauntered down Albumuth, breathing in the smell of catfish simmering on open skillets, the tangy broth of codger soup, the sweet regret of overripe melons, pomegranates, and leechee fruit offered for sale. Stomach grumbling, he stopped long enough to buy a skewer of beef and onions and eat it noisily, afterwards wiping his hands on the back of his pants. He leaned against a lamp post next to a sidewalk barber and — breathing in the sour effluvium from the shampoos, standing clear of the trickle of water that crept into the gutter — pulled out the map he had bought at *Borges Bookstore*. It was cheaply printed on butcher paper, many of the street names drawn by hand. Colorless, it compared unfavorably with Dvorak's tattoo, but it was accurate and he easily found the intersection of streets that marked his hostel. Beyond the hostel lay the valley of the city proper; north of it stood the religious district and his old teacher, Cadimon Signal. He could make his way to the hostel via one of two routes. The first would take him through an old factory district, no doubt littered with the corpses of rusted out motored vehicles and railroad cars, railroad tracks cut up and curving into the air with a profound sense of futility. In his childhood in the city of Morrow, Dradin, along with his long-lost friend Anthony Toliver (Tolive the Olive, he had been called, because of his fondness for the olive fruit or its oil), had played in just such a district, and it did not fit his temperament. He remembered how their play had been made somber by the sight of the trains, their great, dull heads upended, some staring glassily skyward while others drank in the cool, dark earth beneath. He was in no mood for such a death of metal, not with his heartbeat slowing and rushing, his manner at once calm and hyperactive.

No, he would take the second route — through the oldest part of the city, over one thousand years old, so old as to have lost any recollection of itself, its stones worn smooth and memory-less by the years. Perhaps such a route would settle him, allow him this bursting joy in his heart and yet not make his head spin quite so much.

Dradin moved on — ignoring an old man defecating on the sidewalk (trousers down around his ankles) and neatly sidestepping an Occidental woman around whom flopped live carp as she, armed with a club, methodically beat at their heads until a spackle of yellow brains glistened on the cobblestones.

AFTER A FEW minutes of walking, the wall-to-wall buildings fell away, taking the smoke and dust and babble of voices with them. The world became a silent place except for the scuff of Dradin's shoes on the cobblestones and the occasional muttering chug-chuff of a motored vehicle, patched up and trundling along, like as not burning more oil than fuel. Dradin ignored the smell of fumes, the angry retort of tailpipes. He saw only the face of the woman from the window — in the pattern of lichen on a gray-stained wall, in the swirl of leaves gathered in a gutter.

Dradin, In Love

The oldest avenues, thoroughfares grandfatherly when the Court of the Mourning Dog had been young and the Days of the Burning Sun had yet to scorch the land, lay a-drowning in a thick soup of honeysuckle, passion fruit, and bougainvillea, scorned by bee and hornet. Such streets had the lightest of traffic: old men on an after-lunch constitutional; a private tutor leading two children dressed in Sunday clothes, all polished shoes and handkerchief-and-spit cleaned faces.

The buildings Dradin passed were made of a stern, impervious gray stone, and separated by fountains and courtyards. Weeds and ivy smothered the sides of these stodgy, baroque halls, their windows broken as if the press of vines inward had smashed the glass. Morning glories, four o'clocks, and yet more ivy choked moldering stone street markers, trailed from rusted balconies, sprouted from pavement cracks, and stitched themselves into fences or gates scoured with old fire burns. Who such buildings had housed, or what business had been conducted within, Dradin could only guess. They had, in their height and solidity, an atmosphere of states-craft about them, bureaucratic in their flourishes and busts, gargoyles and stout columns. But a bureaucracy lost to time: sword-wielding statues on horseback overgrown with lichen, the features of faces eaten away by rot deep in the stone; a fountain split down the center by the muscular roots of an oak. There was such a staggering sense of lawlessness in the silence amid the creepers.

Certainly the jungle had never concealed such a cornucopia of assorted fungus, for between patches of stone burned black Dradin now espied rich clusters of mushrooms in as many colors as there were beggars on Albumuth Boulevard: emerald, magenta, ruby, sapphire, plain brown, royal purple, corpse white. They ranged in size from a thimble to an obese eunuch's belly.

Such a playful and random dotting delighted Dradin so much that he began to follow the spray of mushrooms as much as he could without abandoning his general direction.

Their trail led him to a narrow avenue blocked in by ten-foot high gray stone walls, and he was soon struck by the notion that he travelled down the throat of a serpent. The mushrooms proliferated, until they not only grew in the cobblestone cracks, but also from the walls, speckling the gray with their bright hoods and stems.

The sun dimmed between clouds. A wind came up, brisk on Dradin's face. Trees loured ever closer, darkening the sky ever more. The street continued to narrow until it was wide enough for two men, then one man, and finally so narrow — narrow as any narthex Dradin had ever encountered — that he moved sideways crablike, and still tore a button.

Eventually, the street widened again. He stumbled out into the open space — only to be met by a *crack!* loud as the severing of a spine, a sound that shot up, over, and past him. He cried out and flinched, one arm held up to ward off a blow, as a sea of wings thrashed toward the sky.

He slowly brought his arm down. Pigeons. A flock of pigeons. Only pigeons.

Ahead, when the flock had cleared the trees, Dradin saw, along the street's right hand side, the rotting columbary from which the birds had flown. Its many covey holes had the bottomless gaze of the blind. The stink of pigeon droppings made his stomach queasy. Beside the columbary, separated by an alleyway, stood a columbarium, also rotting and deserted, so that urns of ashes teetered on the edge of a windowsill, while below the smashed window two urns lay cracked on the cobblestones, their black ash spilling out.

A columbary and a columbarium! Side by side, no less, like old and familiar friends, joined in decay.

Much as the sight intrigued him, the alley between the columbary and columbarium fascinated Dradin more, for the mushrooms that had crowded the crevices of the street and dotted the walls like the pox now proliferated beyond all imagining, the cobblestones thick with them in a hundred shades and hues. Down the right hand side of the alley, ten alcoves

Dradin, In Love

had been carved, complete with *fleur d' lis* gates, a hundred hardened cherubim and devils alike caught in the metalwork. The gate of the nearest alcove stood open and from within spilled lichen, creepers, and mushroom dwellers, their red flags droopy. Surrounded by the vines, the mushroom dwellers resembled human headstones or dreamy, drowning swimmers in a green sea.

Beside Dradin — and he jumped back as he realized his mistake — lay a mushroom dweller which he had thought was a mushroom the size of a small child. It mewled and writhed in half-awakened slumber as Dradin looked at it with a mixture of fascination and distaste. Stranger to Ambergris that he was, still Dradin knew of the mushroom dwellers, for, as Cadimon Signal had taught him in Morrow, "they form the most outlandish of all known cults," although little else had been forthcoming from Cadimon's dried and withered lips.

Mushroom dwellers smelled of old, rotted barns and spoiled milk, and vegetables mixed with the moistness of dark crevices and the dryness of day-dead dung beetles. Some folk said they whispered and plotted among themselves in a secret language so old that no one else, even in the far, far Occident, spoke it. Others said they came from the subterranean caves and tunnels below Ambergris, that they were escaped convicts who had gathered in the darkness and made their own singular religion and purpose, that they shunned the light because they were blind from their many years underground. And yet others, the poor and the under-educated, said that newts, golliwogs, slugs, and salamanders followed in their wake by land, while above bats, nighthawks, and whippoorwills flew, feasting on the insects that crawled around mushroom and mushroom dweller alike.

Mushroom dwellers slept on the streets by day, but came out at night to harvest the fungus that had grown in the cracks and shadows of graveyards during sunlit hours. Wherever they slept, they planted the red flags of warning, and woe to the man who, as Dradin had, disturbed their wet and lugubrious slumber. Sailors on the docks had told Dradin that the mushroom dwellers were known to rob graves for compost, or even murder tourists and use the flesh for their midnight crop. If no one questioned or policed them, it was because during the night they tended to the garbage and carcasses that littered Ambergris. By dawn the streets had been picked clean and lay shining and innocent under the sun.

FIFTY MUSHROOM DWELLERS now spilled out from the alcove gateway, macabre in their very peacefulness and the even hum-thrum of their breath: stunted in growth, wrapped in robes the pale gray-green of a frog's underbelly, their heads hidden by wide-brimmed gray felt hats that, like the hooded tops of their namesakes, covered them to the neck. Their necks were the only exposed part of them — incredibly long, pale necks; at rest, they did indeed resemble mushrooms.

And yet, to Dradin's eye, they were disturbingly human rather than inhuman — a separate race, developing side by side, silent, invisible, chained to ritual — and the sight of them, on the same day that he had fallen so irrevocably in love, unnerved Dradin. He had already felt death upon him in the jungles and had known no fear, only pain, but here fear burrowed deep into his bones. Fear of death. Fear of the unknown. Fear of knowing death before he drank deeply of love. Morbidity and sullen curiosity mixed with dreams of isolation and desolation. All those obsessions of which the religious institute had supposedly cured him.

Positioned as he was, at the mouth of the alley, Dradin felt as though he were spying on a secret, forbidden world. Did they dream of giant mushrooms, gray caps agleam with the dark light of a midnight sun? Did they dream of a world lit only by the phosphorescent splendor of their charges?

Dradin watched them for a moment longer and then, his pace considerably faster, made his way past the alley mouth.

Dradin, In Love

EVENTUALLY, UNDER THE cloud-darkened eye of the sun, the maze of alleys gave way to wide, open-ended streets traversed by carpenters, clerks, blacksmiths, and broadsheet vendors, and he soon came upon the depressing but cheap Holander-Barth Hostel. (In another, richer, time he never would have considered staying there.) He had seen all too many such establishments in the jungles: great mansions rotted down to their foundations, occupied by the last inbred descendants of men and women who had thought the jungle could be conquered with machete and fire, only to find that the jungle had conquered them; where yesterday they had hacked down a hundred vines a thousand now writhed and interlocked in a fecundity of life. Dradin could not even be sure that the Sisters of Mercy Hospital still stood, untouched by such natural forces.

The Holander-Barth Hostel, once white, now dull gray, was a salute to pretentiousness, the dolorous inlaid marble columns crumbling from the inside out and laundry spread across ornately filigreed balconies black with decay. Perhaps once, a long time ago, jaded aristocrats had owned it, but now tubercular men walked its halls, hacking their lungs out while fishing in torn pockets for cigars or cigarettes. The majority were soldiers from long-forgotten campaigns who had used their pensions to secure lodging, blissfully ignorant (or ignoring) the cracked fixtures, curled wall paper, communal showers and toilets. But, as the hansom driver had remarked on the way in, "It is the cheapest" and had added, "It is also far away from the festival." Luckily, the proprietors respected a man of the cloth, no matter how weathered, and Dradin had managed to rent one of two second story rooms with a private bath.

Heart pounding now not from fear, but rather from desire, Dradin dashed up the warped veranda — past the elderly pensioners, who bowed their heads or made confused signs of the cross — up the spiral staircase, came to his door, fumbled with the key, and once inside, fell on the bed with a thump that made the springs groan, the book thrown down beside him. The cover felt velvety and smooth to his touch. It felt like her skin must feel, he thought, and promptly fell asleep, a smile on his lips, for it was still near midday and the heat had drained his strength.

Thus began the fantasy: that, in some other room, some other house — perhaps even in the valley below — the woman from the window lay on her own bed by some dim light and turned these same pages

III.

MOUTH DRY, HAIR tousled, and chin scratchy with stubble, Dradin woke to a pinched nerve in his back that made him moan and turn over and over on the bed, his perspective notably skewed, though not this time by the woman. Still, he could tell that the sun had plummeted beneath the horizon, and where the sky had been gray with clouds, it now ranged from black to a bruised purple, the moon mottled, the light measured out in rough dollops. Dradin yawned and scrunched his shoulders together to cure the pinchedness, then rose and walked to the tall but slender windows. He unhooked the latch and pulled the twin panes open to let in the smell of approaching rain, mixed with the sweet stink of garbage and honeysuckle.

The window looked down on the city proper, which lay inside the cupped hands of a valley veined with tributaries of the Moth. It was there that ordinary people slept and dreamt not of jungles and humidity and the lust that fed and starved men's hearts, but of quiet walks under the stars and milk-fat kittens and the gentle hum of wind on wooden porches. They raised families and doubtless missionaries never moved amongst their ranks, but only full-fledged priests, for *they* were already converted to a faith. Indeed, *they* — and people like them in other cities — paid their tithes and, in return, had emissaries sent out into the wilderness to spread the word, such emissaries nothing more than the physical form of their own hopes, wishes, fears; *yea, their desires made flesh*. Dradin found the idea a sad one, sadder still, in a way he hesitated to define, that were it not for his chosen vocation, he could have had such a life: settling down into a daily rhythm that did not include the throbbing of the jungles, twinned to the beating of his heart. Anthony Toliver had chosen such a life, abandoning the clergy soon after graduation from the religious institute.

Around the valley lay the fringe, like a roughly circular smudge of wine and vulgar lipstick. The Holander-Barth Hostel marked the dividing line between the valley and fringe, just as the beginning of Albumuth Boulevard marked the end of the docks and the beginning of the fringe. It was here, not truly at a city's core, that Dradin had always been most comfortable, even back in his religious institute days, when he had been more severe on himself than the most pious monks who taught him.

On the fringe, jesters pricked and pranced, jugglers plied their trade with babies and knives (mixing the two as casually as one might mix apples and oranges). The life's blood swelled at a more exhilarating pace, a pace that quickened beyond the fringe, where the doughty sailors of the River Moth sailed on barges, dhows, frigates, and the rare steamer: anything that could float and hold a man without sinking into the silt.

Beyond the river lay the jungles, where the pace quickened into madness. The jungles hid creatures that died after a single day, their lives condensed beyond comprehension, so that Dradin, in observation of their own swift mortality, had sensed his body dying, hour by hour, minute by minute, a feeling that had not left him even when he lay down with the sweaty woman priest.

Dradin, In Love

Dradin let the breeze from the window brush against him, cooling him, then returned to the bed, circling around it to the bedlamp, turned the switch, and lo!, a brassy light to read by. He plopped down on the bed, legs akimbo, and opened the book to the first page. Thus began the fantasy: that in some other room, some other house — perhaps even in the valley below — the woman from the window lay in her own bed by some dim light and turned these same pages, read these same words. The touch of the pages to his fingers was erotic; they felt damp and charged his limbs with the short, sharp shock of a ceremonial cup of liqueur. He became hard, but resisted the urge to touch himself. Ah, sweet agony! Nothing in his life had ever felt half so good, half so tortuous. Nothing in the bravely savage world beyond the Moth could compare: not the entwining snake dances of the Magpie Women of the Frangipani Veldt, nor the single, aching cry of a Zinfendel maid as she jumped headfirst into the roar of a waterfall. Not even the sweaty woman priest before the fever struck, her panting moans during their awkward love play more a testimonial to the humidity and ever-present mosquitoes than any skill on his part.

Dradin looked around his room. How bare it was for all that he had lived some thirty years. There was his red-handled machete, balanced against the edge of the dresser drawers, and his knapsack, which contained powders and liquids to cure a hundred jungle diseases, and his orange-scuffed boots beside that, and his coins on the table, the gold almost crimson in the light, but what else? Just his suitcase with two changes of clothes, his yellowing, torn diploma from the Morrow Institute of Religiosity, and daguerreotypes of his mother and father, them in their short-lived youth, Dad not yet a red-faced, broken-veined lout of an academic, Mom's eyes not yet squinty with surrounding wrinkles and sharp as bloodied shards of glass.

What did the woman's room look like? No doubt it too was briskly clean, but not bare, oh no. It would have a bed with white mosquito netting and a place for a glass of water, and her favorite books in a row beside the bed, and beyond that a white and silver mantel and mirror, and below that, her dresser drawers, filled to bursting with frilly night things and frilly day things, and filthily frilly twilight things as well. Powders and lotions for her skin, to keep it beyond the pale. Knitting needles and wool, or other less feminine tools for hobbies. Perhaps she kept a vanilla kitten close by, to play with the balls of wool. If she lived at home, this might be the extent of her world, but if she lived alone, then Dradin had three, four, other rooms to fill with her loves and hates. Did she enjoy small talk and other chatter? Did she dance? Did she go to social events? What might she be thinking as she read the book, on the first page of which was written:

> THE REFRACTION OF LIGHT IN A PRISON
> *(Being an Account of the Truffidian Monks
> Held in the Dungeons of the Kalif,
> For They Have Not Given Up Sanity, Nor Hope)*
>
> BY:
> Brother Peek
> Brother Prowcosh
> Brother Witamoor
> Brother Sirin
> Brother Grae
>
> (and, held unfortunately in separate quarters,
> communicating to us purely
> by the force of her will, Sister Stalker)

And, on the next page:

> BEING CHAPTER ONE:
> THE MYSTICAL PASSIONS
>
> *The most mystical of all passions are those practiced by the water people of the Lower Moth, for though they remain celibate and spend most of their lives in the water, they attain a oneness with their mates that bedevils those lesser of us who equate love with intercourse. Surely their women would never become the objects of their desire, for then these women would lose an intrinsic eroticism.*

Dradin, In Love

Dradin read on impatiently, his hands sweaty, his throat dry, but, no, no, he would not rise to drink water from the sink, nor release his tension, but must burn, as his love must burn, reading the self-same words. For now he was in truth a missionary, converting himself to the cause of love, and he could not stop.

Outside, along the lip of the valley, lights began to blink and waver in phosphorescent reds, greens, blues, and yellows, and Dradin realized that preparations for the Festival of the Fresh Water Squid must be underway. On the morrow night, Albumuth Boulevard would be cleared for a parade that would overflow onto the adjacent streets and then the entire city. Along the avenues, candles wrapped in boxes of crepe paper would appear, so that the light would be like the dancing of the squid, great and small, upon the midnight salt water where it met the mouth of the Moth. A celebration of the spawning season, when males battled mightily for females of the species and the fisherfolk of the docks would set out for a month's trawling of the lusting grounds, hoping to bring back enough meat to last until winter.

If only, Dradin thought, if only he could be with her on the morrow night. Among the sights the hansom driver had pointed out on the way into Ambergris was a tavern, *The Drunken Boat*, decked out with the finest in cutlery and clientele, and featuring, for the festival only, the caterwauling of a band called The Ravens. To dance with her, her hands interwoven with his, the scent of her body on his, would make up for all that had happened in the jungle and the humiliations since: the hunt for ever more miserable jobs, accompanied by a general lightening of coin in his pockets.

The clocks struck the insomniac hours after midnight and, below the window, Dradin heard the moist scuttle of mushroom dwellers as they gathered offal and refuse. Rain followed the striking of the clocks, falling softly, as light in touch as Dradin's hand upon *The Refraction of Light in a Prison*. The smell of rain, fresh and sharp, came from the window.

Drawn by that smell, Dradin put the book aside and rose to the window, watched the rain as it caught the faint light, the drops like a school of tiny silver-scaled fish, here and gone, back a moment later. There was a vein of lightning, a boom of thunder, and the rain came faster and harder.

Many times Dradin had stared through the rain-splashed windows of the old gray house on the hill from his childhood in Morrow (the house with the closed shutters like eyes stitched shut) while relatives came up the gray, coiled road: the headlights of expensive motored vehicles bright in the sheen of rain as they appeared suddenly from the haze of fog. They resembled a small army of hunched black, white, and red beetles, like the ones in his father's insect books, creeping up the hill. Below them, where it was not fogged over, Dradin could see the rest of Morrow: industrious, built of stone and wood, feeding off of the River Moth.

From one particular window in the study, Dradin could enjoy a double image: inside, at the end of a row of three open doors — library, living room, dining room — his enormous opera singer of a mother (tall and big-boned, her face carved from stone) stuffed into the kitchen. No maid helped her, for they lived, the three of them, alone on the hill, and so she would be delicately placing mincemeats on plates, cookies on trays, splashing lemonade and punch into glasses, trying very hard to keep her hands clean and her red dress of frills and lace unstained. She would sing to herself as she worked, in an unrestrained and husky voice (it seemed she never spoke to Dradin, but only sang) so that he could hear, conducted through the various pipes, air ducts, and passageways, the words of Voss Bender's greatest opera:

> *Come to me in the Spring*
> *When the rains fall hard*
> *For you are sweet as pollen,*
> *Sweet as fresh honeycomb.*

Dradin, In Love

When the hard brown branches
Of the oak sprout green leaves,
In the season of love, come to me.

Into the oven would go the annual pheasant, while outside the window Dradin could see his father, thin and meticulous in a tuxedo and tails, picking his way through the puddles in the front drive, carrying a big, ragged black umbrella, the spokes harried and buffeted by the wind. Dad would walk *precisely*, as if by stepping first *here* and then *there*, he might escape the rain drops, slip between them because he knew the umbrella would do no good, riddled as it was with rips and moth holes. But, oh, what a pantomime for the guests!, while Dradin laughed and his mother sang. Apologies for the rain, the puddles, the tattered appearance of the umbrella. In later years, Dad's greetings became loutish, slurred by drink and age until they were no longer generous but monstrous. But back then he would unfold his limbs like a good-natured mantis and with quick movements of his hands switch the umbrella from left to right as he gestured his apologies. All the while, the guests would be half-in, half-out of the car — Aunt Sophie and Uncle Ken, perhaps — trying hard to be polite, but meanwhile drenched to the skin. Inside, Mom would have time to steel herself, ready a greeting smile by the front door, and — one doomful eye on the soon-to-be-burnt pheasant — call for Dradin.

IN A MUCH more raging rain, Dradin had first been touched by a force akin to the spiritual. It occurred on a similarly dreary day of visiting relatives, Dradin only nine and trapped: trapped by dry pecks on the cheek; trapped by the smell of damp, sweaty bodies brought close together; trapped by the dry burn of cigars and by the alarming stares of the elderly men, eyebrows inert white slugs, moustaches wriggly, eyes enormous and watery through glasses or monocles. Trapped, too, by the ladies, even worse at that advanced age, their cavernous grouper mouths intent on devouring him whole into their swollen bellies.

Dradin had begged his mother to invite Anthony Toliver and, against his father's wishes, she had said yes. Anthony, a fearless follower, was a wiry boy with sallow skin and dark eyes. They had met in public school, odd fellows bonded together by the simple fact that both had been beaten up by the school bully, Roger Gimmell.

As soon as Tony arrived, Dradin convinced him to escape the party. Off they snuck, through a parlor door into the backyard, a backyard without a fence that went on forever, bounded only at the horizon by a tangled wilderness of trees.

Into the rain they snuck. Water pelted them, splattered on shirts, and pummeled flesh, so that Dradin's ears rang with the force of it and dull aches woke him the morning after. Grass was swept away, dirt dissolving into mud.

Tony fell almost immediately and, scrabbling at Dradin, made him fall too, into the wet, grasping at weeds for support. Tony laughed at the surprised look on Dradin's face. Dradin laughed at the mud clogging Tony's left ear. Splash! Slosh! Mud in the boots, mud in the trousers, mud flecking their hair, mud coating their faces.

As they grappled and giggled, the rain fell so hard it stung. It bit into their clothes, cut into the tops of their heads, attacked their eyes so they could barely open them. In the middle of the mud fight they stopped battling each other and started battling the rain. They scrambled to their feet, no longer playing, then lost touch with each other, Tony's hand slipping from Dradin's, so that Tony said only, "Come on!" and ran toward the house, never looking back at Dradin, who stood still as a frightened rabbit, utterly alone in the universe.

As Dradin stands alone in the sheets of rain, staring at the heavens that have opened up and sent the rains down, he begins to shake from a feeling deep within him. The rain, like a hand on his shoulders, presses him down; the electric sensation of water on his skin rinses away mud and bits of grass, leaves him cold and sodden. He shudders convulsively, sensing the prickle of an immensity up in the sky, staring down at him. He knows from the rush and rage of blood within him, the magnified beat of his heart, that nothing this *alive*, this out of control, can be random.

Dradin closes his eyes and a thousand colors, a thousand images, explode inside his mind, one for each drop of rain. A rain of shooting stars, and from this conflagration the universe opening up before him. For an instant, Dradin can sense every throbbing artery and arrhythmic heart in the city below him — every darting quicksilver thought of hope, of pain, of hatred, of love. A hundred thousand sorrows and a hundred thousand joys ascending to him.

The babble of sensation so overwhelms him that he can hardly breathe, cannot feel his body except as a hollow receptacle. Then the sensations fade until, closer at hand, he feels the pinprick lives of mice in the nearby glades, the deer like graceful shadows, the foxes clever in their burrows, the ladybugs hidden on the undersides of leaves, and then nothing, and when it is gone, he says, shoulders slumped, but still on his feet, *Is this God?*

When Dradin — a husk now, his hearing deafened by the rain, his bones cleansed by it — turned back toward the house; when he finally faced the house with its shuttered windows, as common sense dictated he should, the light from within fairly burst to be let out. And Dradin saw (as he stood by the window in the hostel) not Tony, who was safely inside, but his mother. His mother. The later memory fused to the earlier seamlessly, as if they had happened together, one, of a piece. That he had turned and she was there, already leveling a blank stare toward him; that, simple as breath, the rain brought redemption and madness crashing down on both their heads, the time span no obstacle and of no importance.

. . . he turned and there was his mother, on her knees in the mud, in her red dress spattered brown. She scooped the mud up with her hands, regarded it, and began to eat, so ravenously that she bit into her little finger. The eyes on the face of stone — the face as blank as the rain — looked up at him with the most curious expression, as if trapped as Dradin had felt trapped inside the house, trapped and asking Dradin . . . to do something. And him, even then, already fourteen, not knowing what to do, calling for Dad, calling for a doctor, while the mud smudged the edges of her mouth and, unconcerned, she ate more and stared at him after each bite, until he cried and came to her and hugged her and tried to make her stop, though nothing in the world could make her stop, or make him stop trying. What unnerved him more than anything, more than the mud in her mouth, was the complete silence that surrounded her, for he had come to define her by her voice, and this she did not use, even to ask for help.

DRADIN AGAIN HEARD the mushroom dwellers below and closed the window abruptly. He sat back on the bed. He wanted to read more of the book, except that now his thoughts floated, rose and fell like waves and, before he realized it, before he could stop it, he was, as it were, not quite dead, but merely asleep.

***

IN THE MORNING Dradin rose rested and spry, his body almost certainly recovered from the jungle fever. For months he had risen to the ache of sore muscles and bruised internal organs; now he had only a fever of a different sort. Every time Dradin glanced at *The Refraction of Light in a Prison* — as he washed his face in the green-tinged basin, as he dressed, not looking at his pant legs so it took him several tries to put them on — he thought of her. What piece of glitter might catch her

Dradin, In Love

eye for him? For now, surely, if she had read the book, was the time to appraise her worth to him, to let her know that serious is as serious does. In just such a manner had his dad wooed his mom, Dad a rake-thin but puff-bellied proud graduate of Morrow's University of Arts & Facts (which certainly defined Dad). She, known by the maiden name of Barsombly, the famous singer with a voice like a pit bull — almost baritone, but husky enough, Dradin admitted, to conceal a sultry sexuality. He could not remember when he had not either felt the *thrulling* vibrations of his mother's voice or heard the voice itself. Or a time when he had not watched as she applied raucous perfumes and powders to herself, after putting on the low-bodiced, gold-satin costumes that rounded her taut bulk like an impenetrable wall. He could remember her taking him into theatres and music halls through the back entrance, bepuddled and muddened, and as some helpful squire would escort him sodden to his seat, so too would she be escorted atop the stage, so that as Dradin sat, the curtain rose, simultaneous with the applause from the audience — an ovation like the crashing of waves against rocks.

Then she would sing, and he would imagine the thrull of her against him, and marvel at the power of her voice, the depths and hollows of it, the way it matched the flow and melody of the orchestra only to diverge, coursing like a secret and perilous undertow, the vibration growing and growing until there was no longer any music at all, but only the voice devouring the music.

Dad did not go to any of her performances and sometimes Dradin thought she sang so loud, so full of rage, that Dad might still hear her faintly, him up late reading in the study of the old house on the hill with the shutters like eyes stitched shut.

His mother would have been proud of his attempts to woo, but, alas, she had been gagged and trussed for her own good and travelled now with the Bedlam Rovers, a cruising troupe of petty psychiatrists — sailing down the Moth on a glorified houseboat under the subtitle of "Boat Bound Psychiatrists: Miracle Workers of the Mind" — to whom, finally, Dad had given over his dearest, the spiced fig of his heart, Dradin's mother — for a fee, of course; and didn't it, Dad had raged and blustered, come to the same thing? In a rest home or asylum; either situated in one place, or on the move. It was not so bad, he would say, slumping down in a damp green chair, waving his amber bottle of Smashing Ted's Finest; after all, the sights she would see, the places she would experience, and all under the wise and benevolent care of trained psychiatrists who *paid* to take that care. Surely, his father would finish with a belch or burp, there is no better arrangement.

Youngish Dradin, still smarting from the ghost of the strap of a half an hour past dared not argue, but thought often: yes, but all such locutions of thought are reliable and reliant upon one simple supposition — to whit, that she be insane. What if not insane but sane "south by southwest" as the great Voss Bender said? What if, inside the graying but leopardesque head, the burgeoning frame, lay a wide realm of sanity, with only the outer shell susceptible to hallucinations, incantations, and inappropriate metaphors? What then? To be yanked about thus, like an animal on a chain, could this be stood by a sane individual? Might such parading and humiliation lead a person to the very insanity hitherto avoided?

And, worse thought still, that his father had driven her to it with his cruel, carefully-planned indifference.

But Dradin — remembering the awful silence of that day in the rain when Mom had stuffed her mouth full of mud — refused to dwell on it. He must find a present for his darling, this accomplished by rummaging through his pack and coming up with a necklace, the centerpiece an uncut emerald. It had been given to him by a tribal chieftain as a bribe to go away ("There is only One God," Dradin said. "What's his name?" the chieftain asked. "God," replied Dradin. "How bloody boring," the chieftain said. "Please go away.") and he had taken it initially as a donation to the Church, although he had meant to give it to the spiced fig of his heart, the sweaty woman priest, only to have the fever overtake him first. As he held the necklace in his hand, he recognized the exceptional workmanship of the blue-and-green beads. If he were to sell it, he might pay the rent at the hostel for another week. But, more attractive, if he gave it to his love, she would understand the seriousness of his heart's desire.

With uncharacteristic grace and a touch of inspired lunacy, Dradin tore the first page from *The Refraction of Light in a Prison* and wrote his name below the name of the last monk, like so:

Brother Dradin Kashmir -
Not truly a brother, but devout
in his love for you alone

There. It was done. It could not be undone. Dradin looked over his penmanship with satisfaction. Now he could have an unhurried breakfast at the hostel restaurant.

In the jungle deaths occurred in such thick numbers that one might walk a mile on the decayed carcasses, the white clean bones of deceased animals

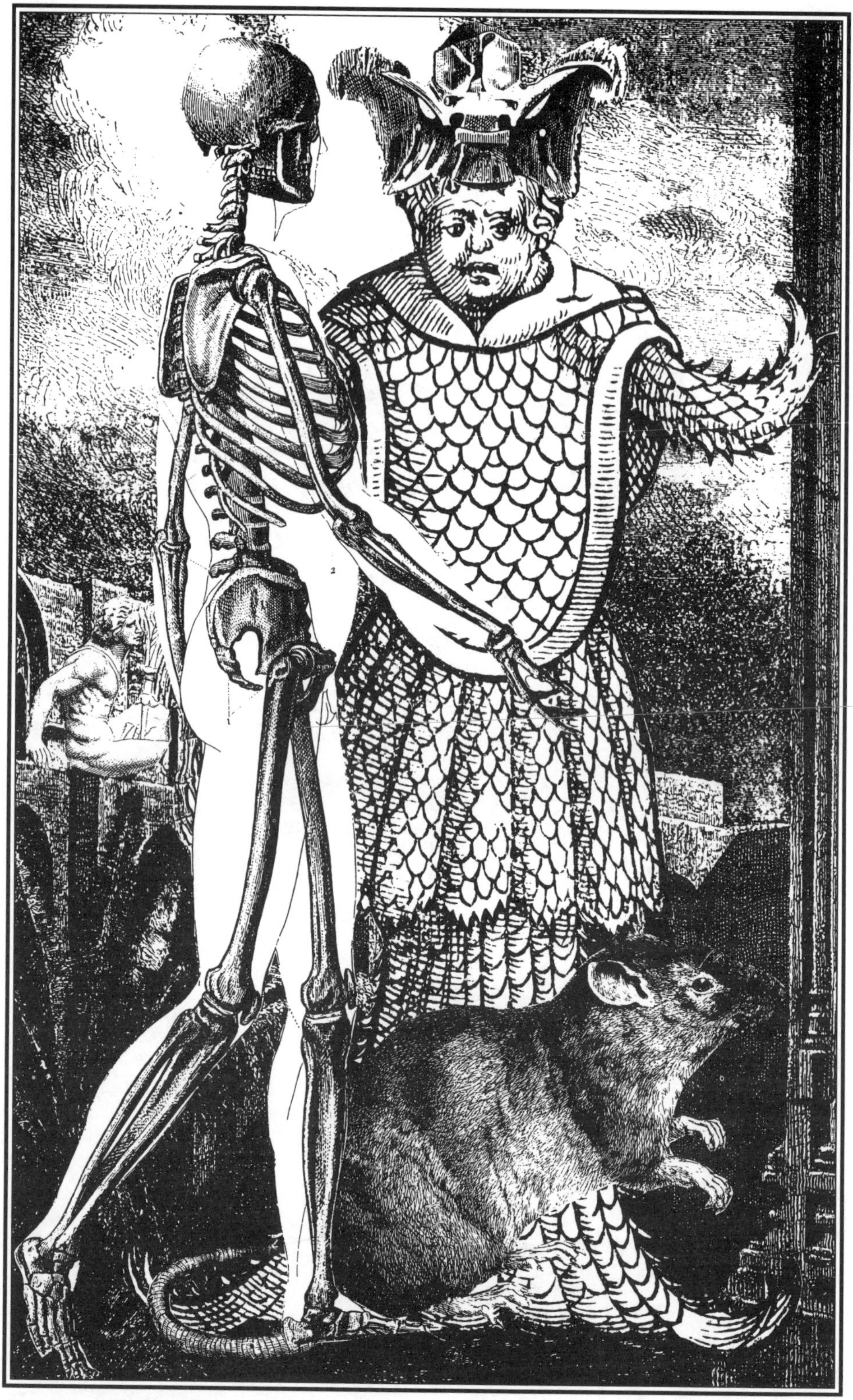

IV.

OVER BREAKFAST, HIS sparse needs tended to by a gaunt waiter who looked like a malaria victim, Dradin examined his dull gray map. Toast without jam for him, nothing richer like sausages frying in their own fat, or bacon with white strips of lard. The jungle climate had, from the start, made his bowels and bladder loosen up and pour forth their bile like the sludge of rain in the most deadly of monsoon seasons. Dradin had avoided rich foods ever since, saying no to such jungle delicacies as fried grasshopper, boiled peccary, and a local favorite that baked huge black slugs into their shells.

From dirty gray table-clothed tables on either side, war veterans coughed and harrumphed, their bloodshot eyes perked into semi-awareness by the sight of Dradin's map. Treasure? War on two fronts? Mad, drunken charges into the eyeteeth of the enemy? No doubt. Dradin knew their type, for his father was the same, if with an academic bent. The map would be a mystery of the mind to his father.

Nonetheless, ignoring their stares, Dradin found the religious quarter on the map, traced over it with his index finger. It resembled a bird's eye view of a wheel with interconnecting spokes. No more a "quarter" than drawn. Cadimon Signal's mission stood near the center of the spokes, snuggled into a corner between the Church of the Fisherman and the Cult of the Seven-Edged Star. Even looking at it on the map made Dradin nervous. To meet his religious instructor after such a time. How would Cadimon have aged after seven years? Perversely, as far afield as Dradin had gone, Cadimon Signal had, in that time, come closer to the center, his home, for he had been born in Ambergris. At the religious institute Cadimon had extolled the city's virtues and, to be fair, its vices many times after lectures, in the common hall. His voice, hollow and echoing against the black marble archways, gave a raspy voice to the gossamer-thin cherubim carved into the swirl of white marble ceilings. Dradin had spent many nights along with Anthony Toliver listening to that voice, surrounded by thousands of religious texts on shelves gilded with gold leaf.

The question that most intrigued Dradin, that guided his thoughts and bedeviled his nights, was this: Would Cadimon Signal take pity on a former student and find a job for him? He hoped, of course, for a missionary position, but failing that a position which would not break his back or tie him in knots of bureaucratic red tape. Dad was an unlikely ally in this, for Dad had recommended Dradin to Cadimon and also recommended Cadimon to Dradin.

Before the fuzzy beginnings of Dradin's memory, Dad had, when still young and thin and mischievous, invited Cadimon over for tea and conversation, surrounded in Dad's study by books, books, and more books. Books on culture and civilization, religion and philosophy. They would, or so Dad told Dradin later, debate every topic imaginable, and some that were unimaginable, distasteful, or all too real until the hours struck midnight, one o'clock, two o'clock, and the lanterns dimmed to an ironic light, brackish and ill-suited to discussion. Surely this bond would be enough? Surely Cadimon would look at him and see the father in the son?

Dradin, In Love

AFTER BREAKFAST, NECKLACE and map in hand, Dradin wandered into the religious quarter, known by the common moniker of Pejora's Folly after Midan Pejora, the principal early architect, to whose credit or discredit could be placed the slanted walls, the jumble of Occidental and accidental, northern and southern, baroque and pure jungle, styles. Buildings battled for breath and space like centuries-slow soldiers in brick-to-brick combat. To look into the revolving spin of a kaleidoscope while heavily intoxicated, Dradin thought, would not be half so bad.

The rain from the night before took the form of sunlit droplets on plants, windowpanes, and cobblestones that wiped away the dull and dusty veneer of the city. Cats preened and tiny hop toads hopped while dead sparrows lay in furrows of water, beaten down by the storm's ferocity. Dradin felt fresh and clean, and breathed deeply of the breezy, damp air.

He snorted in disbelief as he observed followers of gentle Saint Solon the Decrepit placing the corpses of rain victims such as the sparrows into tiny wooden coffins for burial. In the jungle deaths occurred in such thick numbers that one might walk a mile on the decayed carcasses, the white clean bones of deceased animals, and after a time even the most fastidious missionary gave the crunching sound not a second thought.

As he neared the mission, Dradin tried to calm himself by breathing in the acrid scent of votive candles burning from alcoves and crevices and balconies. He tried to imagine the richness of his father's conversations with Cadimon — the plethora of topics discussed, the righteous and pious denials and arguments. When his father mentioned those conversations, the man would shake off the weight of years, his voice light and his eyes moist with nostalgia. If only Cadimon remembered such encounters with similar enthusiasm.

The slap-slap of punished pilgrim feet against the stones of the street pulled him from his reverie, and he stood to one side as twenty or thirty mendicants slapped on past, cleansing their sins through their callouses, on their way to one of a thousand shrines. In their calm but blank gaze, their slack mouths, Dradin saw the shadow of his mother's face, and he wondered what she had done while his father and Cadimon talked. Gone to sleep? Finished up the dishes? Sat in bed and listened through the wall?

Above Dradin, from towers and from the windows of a hundred temples and churches and devotionals, came cries to prayer in a hundred tongues, from monotone to baritone to soprano. The chorus of voices reminded him of his days in the academy, as did everything, if he were to be truthful — even the sacred rats, potato sack fat with offerings of pudding and chicken and bread, that waddled back and forth between open-air altars. Cadimon had taught them the use of rats in certain ceremonies, and Tony had even caught a rat once, beneath Dradin's bunk. They had named it Belcher after the nickname of a reviled priest and let it eat table scraps.

At last, Dradin found the Mission of Cadimon Signal. Set back from the street, the mission remained almost invisible among the skyward-straining cathedrals surrounding it — remarkable only for the emptiness, the silence, and the swirl of swallows skimming through the air like weightless trapeze artists. The building that housed the mission was an old tin-roofed warehouse reinforced with mortar and brick, opened up from the inside with ragged holes for skylights, which made Dradin wonder what they did when it rained. Let it rain on them, he supposed.

Christened with fragmented mosaics that depicted saints, monks, and martyrs, the enormous doorway lay open to him. All around, acolytes frantically lifted sandbags and long pieces of timber, intent on barricading the entrance, but none challenged him as he walked up the steps and through the gateway; no one, in fact, spared him a second glance, so focused were they on their efforts.

Dradin, In Love

Inside, Dradin went from sunlight to shadows, his footfalls hollow in the silence. A maze of paths wound through lush green Occidental-style gardens. The gardens centered around rock-lined pools cut through by the curving fins of corpulent carp. Next to the pools lay the eroded ruins of ancient, pagan temples, which had been reclaimed with gaily-colored paper and splashes of red, green, blue, and white paint. Among the temples and gardens and pools, unobtrusive as lamp posts, acolytes in gray habits toiled, removing dirt, planting herbs, and watering flowers. The air had a metallic color and flavor to it and Dradin heard the buzzing of bees at the many poppies, the soft *scull-skithing* as acolytes wielded their scythes against encroaching weeds.

The ragged, blue grass-fringed trail led Dradin to a raised mound of dirt on which stood a catafalque, decorated with gold leaf and the legend "Saint Philip the Philanderer" printed along its side. In the shadow of the catafalque, amid the blue grass, a gardener dressed in dark green robes planted lilies he had set on a nearby bench. Atop the catafalque, halting Dradin in mid-step, stood Signal. He had changed since Dradin had last seen him, for he was bald and gaunt, with white tufts of hair sprouting from his ears. A studded dog collar circled his withered neck. But most disturbing, unless one wished to count a cask of Solomon's Wine that dangled from his left hand — no doubt shipped in by those reliable if questionable purveyors of spirits Hoegbotton & Sons, perhaps even held, caressed, by his love — *the man was stark staring naked!* The object of no one's desire bobbed like a length of flaccid purpling sausage, held in some semblance of erectitude by the man's right hand, the hand currently engaged in an up-and-down motion that brought great pleasure to its owner.

"Ccc-Cadimon Ssss-sigggnal?"

"Yes, who is it now?" said the gardener.

"I beg your pardon."

"I said," repeated the gardener with infinite patience, as if he really would not mind saying it a third, a fourth, or a fifth time, "I said 'Yes, who is it now?' "

"It's Dradin. Dradin Kashmir. Who are you?" Dradin kept one eye on the naked man atop the catafalque.

"I'm Cadimon Signal, of course," the gardener said, patiently pulling weeds, plotting lilies. *Pull, plot, pull.* "Welcome to my mission, Dradin. It's been a long time." The small, green-robed man in front of Dradin had mannerisms and features indistinguishable from any wizened beggar on Ambergris Boulevard, but looking closer, Dradin thought he could see a certain resemblance to the man he had known in Morrow. Perhaps.

"Who is he, then?" Dradin pointed to the naked man, who was now ejaculating into a rose bush.

"He's a Living Saint. A professional holy man. You should remember that from your theology classes. I know I must have taught you about Living Saints. Unless, of course, I switched that with a unit on Dead Martyrs. No other kind, really. That's a joke, Dradin. Have the decency to laugh."

The Living Saint, no longer aroused, but quite tired, lay down on the smooth cool stone of the catafalque and began to snore.

"But what's a Living Saint doing here? And naked?"

"I keep him here to discomfort my creditors who come calling. Lots of upkeep to this place. My, you have changed, haven't you?"

"What?"

"I thought *I* had gone deaf. I said you've changed. Please, ignore my Living Saint. As I said, he's for the creditors. Just trundle him out, have him spill his seed, and they don't come back."

"I've changed?"

"Yes, I've said that already." Cadimon stopped plotting lilies and stood up, examined Dradin from crown to stirrups. "You've been to the jungle. A pity, really. You were a good student."

DRADIN, IN LOVE

"I have come back from the jungle, if that's what you mean. I took fever."

"No doubt. You've changed most definitely. Here, hold a lily bulb for me." Cadimon crouched down once more. *Pull, plot, pull.*

"You seem . . . you seem somehow less imposing. But healthier."

"No, no. You've grown taller, that's all. What are you now that you are no longer a missionary?"

"No longer a missionary?" Dradin said, and felt as if he were drowning, and here they had only just started to talk.

"Yes. Or no. Lily please. Thank you. Blessed things require so much dirt. Good for the lungs exercise is. Good for the soul. How is your father these days? Such a shame about your mother. But how is he?"

"I haven't seen him in over three years. He wrote me while I was in the jungle and he seemed to be doing well."

"Mmmm. I'm glad to hear it. Your father and I had the most wonderful conversations a long time ago. A very long time ago. Why, I can remember sitting up at his house — you just in a crib then, of course — and debating the aesthetic value of the Golden Spheres until — "

"I've come here looking for a job."

Silence. Then Cadimon said, "Don't you still work for—"

"I quit." Emphasis on *quit*, like the pressure on an egg to make it crack just so.

"Did you now? I told you you were no longer a missionary. I haven't changed a whit from those days at the academy, Dradin. You didn't recognize me because you've changed, not I. I'm the same. I do not change. Which is more than you can say for the weather around here."

It was time, Dradin decided, to take control of the conversation. It was not enough to counter-punch Cadimon's drifting dialogue. He bent to his knees and gently placed the rest of the lilies in Cadimon's lap.

"Sir," he said. "I need a position. I have been out of my mind with the fever for three months and now, only just recovered, I long to return to the life of a missionary."

"Determined to stick to a point, aren't you?" Cadimon said. "A point stickler. A stickler for rules. I remember you. Always the sort to be shocked by a Living Saint rather than amused. Rehearsed rather than spontaneous. Oh well."

"Cadimon . . ."

"Can you cook?"

"Cook? I can boil cabbage. I can heat water."

Cadimon patted Dradin on the side of his stomach. "So can a hedgehog, my dear. So can a hedgehog, if pressed. No, I mean cook as in the Cooks of Kalay, who can take nothing more than a cauldron of bilge water and a side of beef three days old and tough as calluses and make a dish so succulent and sweet it shames the taste buds to eat so much as a carrot for days afterwards. You can't cook, can you?"

"What does cooking have to do with missionary work?"

"Oh, ho. I would have thought a jungle veteran would know the answer to that! Ever heard of cannibals? Eh? No, that's a joke. It has nothing to do with missionary work. There." He patted the last of the lilies and rose to sit on the bench, indicating with a wave of the hand that Dradin should join him.

Dradin sat down on the bench next to Cadimon. "Surely, you need experienced missionaries?"

Cadimon shook his head. "We don't have a job for you. I'm sorry. You've changed, Dradin."

"But you and my father . . ." Blood rose to Dradin's face. For he could woo until he turned purple, but without a job, how to fund such adventures in pocketbook as his new love would entail?

"Your father is a good man, Dradin. But this mission is not made of money. I see tough times ahead."

Pride surfaced in Dradin's mind like a particularly ugly crocodile. "I am a good missionary, sir. A very good missionary. I

Dradin, In Love

have been a missionary for over five years, as you know. And, as I have said, I am just now out of the jungle, having nearly died of fever. Several of my colleagues did not recover. The woman. The woman . . ."

But he trailed off, his skin goose-pimpled from a sudden chill. Layeville, Flay, Stern, Thaw, and Krug had all gone mad or died under the onslaught of green, the rain and the dysentery, and the savages with their poison arrows. Only he had crawled to safety, the mush of the jungle floor beneath his chest a-murmur with leeches and dungbugs and "molly twelve-step" centipedes. A trek into and out of hell, and he could not even now remember it all, or wanted to remember it all.

"Paugh! Dying of fever is easy. The jungle is easy, Dradin. I could survive, frail as I am. It's the city that's hard. If you'd only bother to observe, you'd see the air is overripe with missionaries. You can't defecate out a window without fouling a brace of them. The city bursts with them. They think that the festival signals opportunity, but the opportunity is not for them! No, we need a cook, and you cannot cook."

Dradin's palms slickened with sweat, his hands shaking as he examined them. What now? What to do? His thoughts circled and circled around the same unanswerable question: How could he survive on the coins he had yet on his person and still woo the woman in the window? And he must woo her; he did not feel his heart could withstand the blow of *not* pursuing her.

"I am a good missionary," Dradin repeated, looking at the ground. "What happened in the jungle was not my fault. We went out looking for converts, and when I came back the compound was overrun."

Dradin's breaths came quick and shallow and his head felt light. Suffocating, that was it, he was suffocating under the weight of jungle leaves closing over his nose and mouth.

Cadimon sighed and shook his head. In a soft voice he said, "I am not unsympathetic," and held out his hands to Dradin. "How can I explain myself? Maybe I cannot, but let me try.

Perhaps this way: Have you converted the Flying Squirrel People of the western hydras? Have you braved the frozen wastes of Lascia to convert the ice cube-like Skamoo?"

"No."

"What did you say?"

"No!"

"Then we can't use you. At least not now."

Dradin's throat ached and his jaw tightened. Would he have to beg, then? Would he have to become a mendicant himself? On the catafalque, the Living Saint had begun to stir, mumbling in his half-sleep.

Cadimon rose and put his hand on Dradin's shoulder. "If it is any consolation, you were never really a missionary, not even at the religious academy. And you are definitely not a missionary now. You are . . . something else. Extraordinary, really, that I can't put my finger on it."

"You insult me," Dradin said, as if he were the gaudy figurehead on some pompous yacht sailing languid on the Moth.

"That is not my intent, my dear. Not at all."

"Perhaps you could give me money. I could repay you."

"Now *you* insult *me*. Dradin, I cannot lend you money. We have no money. All the money we collect goes to our creditors or into the houses and shelters of the poor. We have no money, nor do we covet it."

"Cadimon," Dradin said. "Cadimon, I'm desperate. I need money."

"If you are desperate, take my advice — leave Ambergris. And before the festival. It's not safe for priests to be on the streets after dark on festival night. There have been so many years of calm. Ha! I tell you, it can't last."

"It wouldn't have to be much money. Just enough to — "

Cadimon gestured toward the entrance. "Beg from your father, not from me. Leave. Leave now."

Dradin, taut muscles and clenched fists, would have obeyed Cadimon out of respect for the memory of authority, but now

DRADIN, IN LOVE

a vision rose into his mind like the moon rising over the valley the night before. A vision of the jungle, the dark green leaves with their veins like spines, like long, delicate bones. The jungle and the woman and all of the dead . . .

"I will not."

Cadimon frowned. "I'm sorry to hear you say that. I ask you again, leave."

Lush green, smothering, the taste of dirt in his mouth; the smell of burning, smoke curling up into a question mark.

"Cadimon, I was your student. You owe me the — "

"Living Saint!" Cadimon shouted. "Wake up, Living Saint."

The Living Saint uncurled himself from his repose atop the catafalque.

"Living Saint," Cadimon said, "dispense with him. No need to be gentle." And, turning to Dradin, "Goodbye, Dradin. I am very sorry."

The Living Saint, spouting insults, jumped from the catafalque and — his penis, purpling and flaccid as a sea anemone, brandished menacingly — ran toward Dradin, who promptly took to his heels, stumbling through the ranks of the gathered acolytes and hearing directly behind him as he navigated the blue grass trail not only the Living Saint's screams of "Piss off! Piss off, you great big baboon!" but also Cadimon's distant shouts of: "I'll pray for you, Dradin. I'll pray for you." And, then, too close, much too close, the unmistakable hot and steamy sound of a man relieving himself, followed by the hands of the Living Saint clamped down on his shoulder blades, and a much swifter exit than he had hoped for upon his arrival, scuffing his fundament, his pride, his dignity.

"And stay out!"

WHEN DRADIN STOPPED running he found himself on the fringe of the religious quarter, next to an emaciated macadamia salesman who cracked jokes like nuts. Out of breath, Dradin put his hands on his hips. His lungs strained for air.

Blood rushed furiously through his chest. He could almost persuade himself that these symptoms were only the aftershock of exertion, not the aftershock of anger and desperation. Actions unbecoming a missionary. Actions unbecoming a gentleman. What might love next drive him to?

Determined to regain his composure, Dradin straightened his shirt and collar, then continued on his way in a manner he hoped mimicked the stately gait of a mid-level clergy member, to whom all such earthly things were beneath and below. But the bulge of red, red veins at his neck, the stiffness of fingers in claws at his sides, these clues gave him away, and knowing this made him angrier still. How dare Cadimon treat him as though he were practically a stranger! How dare the man betray the bond between his father and the church!

More disturbing, where were the agents of order when you needed them? No doubt the city had ordinances against public urination. Although that presupposed the existence of a civil authority, and of this mythic beast Dradin had yet to convince himself. He had not seen a single blue, black, or brown uniform, and certainly not filled out with a body lodged within its fabric, a man who might symbolize law and order and thus give the word flesh. What did the people of Ambergris do when thieves and molesters and murderers traversed the thoroughfares and alleyways, the underpasses and the bridges? But the thought brought him back to the mushroom dwellers and their alcove shrines, and he abandoned it, a convulsion traveling from his chin to the tips of his toes. Perhaps the jungle had not yet relinquished its grip.

Finally, shoulders bowed, eyes on the ground, in abject defeat, he admitted to himself that his methods had been grotesque. He had made a fool of himself in front of Cadimon. Cadimon was not beholden to him. Cadimon had only acted as he must when confronted with the ungodly.

Dradin, In Love

NECKLACE STILL WRAPPED in the page from *The Refraction of Light in a Prison,* Dradin came again to Hoegbotton & Sons, only to find that his love no longer stared from the third floor window. A shock traveled up his spine, a shock that might have sent him gibbering to his mother's side aboard the psychiatrists' houseboat, if not that he was a rational and rationalizing man. How his heart drowned in a sea of fears as he tried to conjure up a thousand excuses: she was out to lunch; she had taken ill; she had moved to another part of the building. Never that she was gone for good, lost as he was lost; that he might never, ever see her face again. Now Dradin understood his father's addiction to sweet-milled mead, beer, wine and champagne, for the woman was his addiction, and he knew that if he had only seen her porcelain-perfect visage as he suffered from the jungle fevers, he would have lived for her sake alone.

The city might be savage, stray dogs might share the streets with grimy urchins whose blank eyes reflected the knowledge that they might soon be covered over, blinded forever, by the same two pennies just begged from some gentleman, and no one in all the fuming, fulminous boulevards of trade might know who actually ran Ambergris — or, if anyone ran it at all, but, like a renegade clock, it ran on and wound itself heedless, empowered by the insane weight of its own inertia, the weight of its own citizenry, stamping one, two, three hundred thousand strong; no matter this savagery in the midst of apparent civilization — still the woman in the window seemed to him more ruly, more disciplined and in control and thus, perversely, malleable to his desire, than anyone Dradin had yet met in Ambergris: this priceless part of the whale, this overbrimming stew of the sublime and the superlative.

It was then that his rescuer came: Dvorak, popping up from betwixt a yardstick of a butcher awaiting a hansom and a jowly furrier draped over with furs of auburn, gray, and white. Dvorak, indeed, dressed all in black, against which the red dots of his tattoo throbbed and, in his jacket pocket, a dove-white handkerchief stained red at the edges. A mysterious, feminine smile decorated his mutilated face.

"She's not at the window," Dradin said.

Dvorak's laugh forced his mouth open wide and wider still, carnivorous in its red depths. "No. She is not at the window. But have no doubt: she is inside. She is a most devout employee."

"You gave her the book?"

"I did, sir." The laugh receded into a shallow smile. "She took it from me like a lady, with hesitation, and when I told her it came from a secret admirer, she blushed."

"Blushed?" Dradin felt lighter, his blood yammering and his head a puff of smoke, a cloud, a spray of cotton candy.

"Blushed. Indeed, sir, a good sign."

Dradin took the package from his pocket and, hands trembling, gave it to the dwarf. "Now you must go back in and find her, and when you find her, give her this. You must ask her to join me at *The Drunken Boat* at twilight. You know the place?"

Dvorak nodded, his hands clasped protectively around the package.

"Good. I will have a table next to the festival parade route. Beg her if you must. Intrigue her and entreat her."

"I will do so."

"U-u-unless you think I should take this gift to her myself?"

Dvorak sneered. He shook his head so that the green of the jungles blurred before Dradin's eyes. "Think, sir. Think hard. Would you have her see you first out of breath, unkempt, and, if I may be so bold, there is a slight smell of *urine*. No, sir. Meet her first at the tavern, and there you shall appear a man of means, at your ease, inviting her to the unraveling of further mysteries."

Dradin looked away. How his inexperience must show. How foolish his suggestions. And yet, also, relief that Dvorak had thwarted his brashness.

"Sir?" Dvorak said. "Sir?"

Dradin forced himself to look at Dvorak. "You are correct, of course. I will see her at the tavern."

"Coins, sir."

"Coins?"

"I cannot live on kindness."

"Yes. Of course. Of course." Damn Dvorak! No compassion there. He stuck a hand into his pants pocket and pulled out a gold coin, which he handed to Dvorak. "Another when you return."

"As you wish. Wait here." Dvorak gave Dradin one last long look and then scurried up the steps, and disappeared into the darkness of the doorway.

Dradin discovered he was bad at waiting. He sat on the curb, got up, crouched to his knees, leaned on a lamp post, scratched at a flea biting his ankle. All the while, he looked up at the blank window and thought: If I had come into the city today, I would have looked up at the third floor and seen nothing and this frustration, this impatience, this *ardor*, would not be practically bursting from me now.

Finally, Dvorak scuttled down the steps with his jacket tails floating out behind him, his grin larger, if that were possible, positively a leer.

"What did she say?" Dradin pressed. "Did she say anything? Something? Yes? No?"

"Success, sir. Success. Busy as she is, devout as she is, she said little, but only that she will meet you at *The Drunken Boat*, though perhaps not until after dusk has fallen. She looked quite favorably on the emerald and the message. She calls you, sir, a gentleman."

A gentleman. Dradin stood straighter. "Thank you," he said. "You have been a great help to me. Here." And he passed another coin to Dvorak, who snatched it from his hand with all the swiftness of a snake.

Jeff VanderMeer

As Dvorak murmured goodbye, Dradin heard him with but one ear, cocooned as he was in a world where the sun always shone bright and uncovered all hidden corners, allowing no shadows or dark and glimmering truths.❧

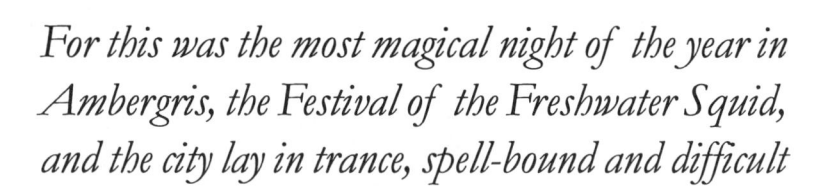

For this was the most magical night of the year in Ambergris, the Festival of the Freshwater Squid, and the city lay in trance, spell-bound and difficult

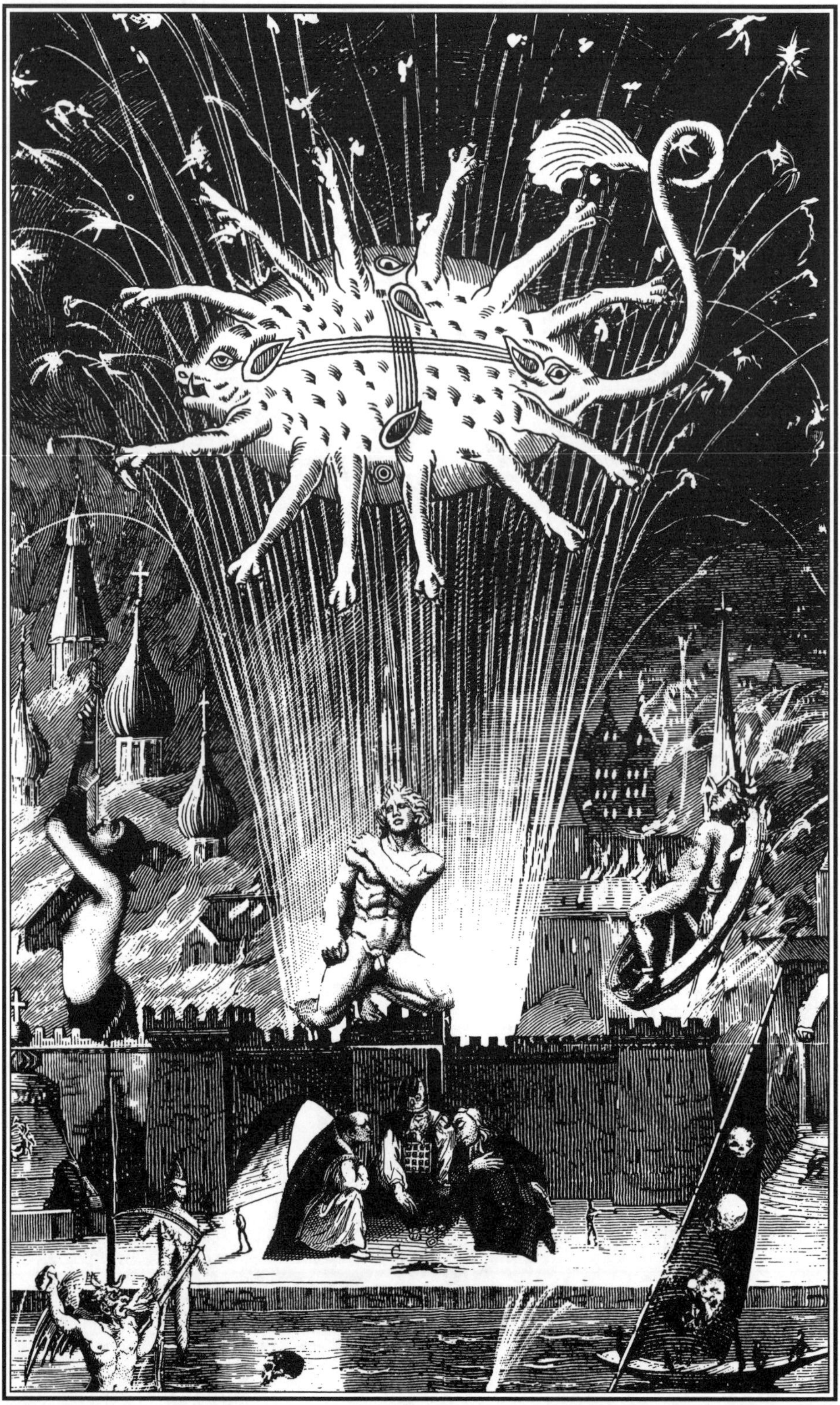

V.

DRADIN HURRIED BACK to the hostel. He hardly saw the flashes of red, green, and blue around him, nor sensed the expectant quality in the air, the huddled groups of people talking in animated voices, for night would bring the Festival of Freshwater Squid and the streets would hum and thrum with celebration. Already, the clean smell of fresh-baked bread, mixed with the treacly promise of sweets, began to tease noses and turn frowns into smiles. Boys let out early from school played games with hoops and marbles and bits of brick. The more adventurous imitated the grand old Kraken sinking ships with a single lash of tentacle, puddle-bound toy boats smashed against drainpipes. Still others watched the erection of scaffolding on tributary streets leading into Albumuth Boulevard. Stiltmen with purpling painted faces hung candy and papier-mache heads in equal quantities from their stilts.

At last, Dradin came to his room, flung open the door, and shut it abruptly behind him. As the citizens of Ambergris prepared for the festival, so now he must prepare for his love, putting aside the distractions of joblessness and decreasing coin.

He stripped and took a shower, turning the water on so hot that needles of heat tattooed his skin red, but he felt clean, and more than clean, cleansed and calm, when he came out after thirty minutes and wiped himself dry with a large green towel. Standing in front of the bathroom mirror in the nude, Dradin noted that although he had filled out since the cessation of his fever, he had not filled out into fat. Not even the shadow of a belly, and his legs thick with muscle. Hardly a family characteristic, that, for his randy father had, since the onset of Mom's river adventures, grown as pudgy as raw bread dough. Nothing for Dad to do but continue to teach ethics at the university and hope that the lithe young things populating his classes would pity him. But for his son a different fate, Dradin was sure.

Dradin shaved, running the blade across his chin and down his neck, so that he thrilled to the self-control it took to keep the blade steady; and yet, when he was done, his hand shook. There. Now various oils worked into the scalp so that his hair became a uniform black, untainted by white except at the outer provinces, where it grazed his ears, and it did not fall back into his face. Then a spot of rouge to bring out the muddy green of his eyes — a scandalous habit, perhaps, learned from his mother of course, but Dradin knew many pale priests who used it.

For clothing, Dradin started with clean underwear and followed with fancy socks done up in muted purple and gold serpent designs. Then the trousers of gray — gray as the slits of his father's eyes in the grip of spirits, gray as his mother's listless moods after performances at the music halls. Yes, a smart gray, a deep gray, not truly conservative, and then the shirt: large on him but not voluminous, white with purple and gold buttons, to match the socks, and a jacket over top that mixed gray and purple thread so that, from heel to head, he looked as distinguished as a debutante at some political gala. It pleased him — as much a uniform as his missionary clothes, but the goal a conversion of a more personal nature. Yes, he would do well.

Dradin, In Love

Thus equipped, his pockets jingly with his last coins, his stomach wrapped in coils of nerves (an at-sea sensation of *notenoughmoney, notenoughmoney* beating inside his organs like a pulse), Dradin made his way out onto the streets.

The haze of twilight had smothered Ambergris, muffling sounds and limiting vision, but everywhere also: lights. Lights from balconies and bedrooms, signposts and horse carriages, candles held by hand and lanterns swinging on the arms of gristled caretakers who sang out, from deep in their throats, "The dying of the light! The dying of the light! Let the Festival begin."

Wraiths riding metal bars, men on bicycles swished past, bells all a-tinkle, and children in formal attire, entow to the vast and long-suffering barges of nannies, who tottered forward on unsteady if stocky legs. Child mimes in white face approached Dradin, prancing and pirouetting, and Dradin clapped in approval and patted their heads. They reminded him of the naked boys and girls of the Nimblytod Tribe, who swung through trees and ate birds that became lost in the forest and could not find their way again into the light.

Women in the red and black of hunter's uniforms crossed his path. They rode hollow wooden horses that fit around their waists, fake wooden legs clacking to either side as their own legs cantered or galloped or pranced, but so controlled, so tight and rigid, that they never broke formation despite the random nature of their movements. The horses had each been individually painted in grotesque shades of green, red, and white: eyes wept blood, teeth snarled into black fangs. The women's lips were drawn back against the red leer of lipstick to neigh and nicker. Around them, the gathering crowd shrieked in laughter, the riders so entranced that only the whites of their eyes showed, shockingly pale against the gloom.

Dradin passed giant spits on which spun and roasted whole cows, whole pigs, and a host of smaller beasts, the spits rotated by grunting, muscular, ruddy-faced men. Everywhere, the mushroom dwellers uncurled from slumber with a yawn, picked up their red flags, and trundled off to their secret and arcane rites. Armed men mock-fought with sabre and with knife while youths wrestled half-naked in the gutters — their bodies burnished with sweat, their eyes focused not on each other but on the young women who watched their battles. Impromptu dances devoid of form or unified steps spread amongst the spectators until Dradin had to struggle through their spider's webs of gyrations, inured to the laughter and chatter of conversations, the tap and stomp of feet on the rough stones. For this was the most magical night of the year in Ambergris, the Festival of the Freshwater Squid, and the city lay in trance, spellbound and difficult, and everywhere, into the apparent lull, glance met glance, eyes sliding from eyes, as if to say, "What next? What will happen next?"

AT LAST, AFTER passing through an archway strung with nooses, Dradin came out onto a main boulevard, *The Drunken Boat* before him. How could he miss it? It had been lit up like an ornament so that all three stories of slanted dark oak decks sparkled and glowed with good cheer.

    A crowd had lined up in front of the tavern, waiting to gain entrance, but Dradin fought through the press, bribed the doorman with a gold coin, and ducked inside, climbing stairs to the second level, high enough to see far down the boulevard, although not so high that the sights would be uninvolving and distant. A tip to the waiter secured Dradin a prime table next to the railing of the deck. The table, complete with lace and embroidered tablecloth, engraved cutlery, and a quavery candle encircled by glass, lay equidistant from the parade and the musical meanderings of The Ravens, four scruffy-looking musicians who played, respectively, the mandolin, twelve-string guitar, the flute, and the drums:

Dradin, In Love

In the city of lies
I spoke in nothing
but the language of spies.

In the city of my demise
I spoke in nothing
but the language of flies.

Their music reminded Dradin of high tide crashing against cliffs and, then, on the down-tempo, of the back-and-forth swell of giant waves rippling across a smooth surface of water. It soothed him and made him seasick both, and when he sat down at the table, the wood beneath him lurched, though he knew it was only the surging of his own pulse, echoed in the floorboards.

Dradin surveyed the parade route, which was lined with glittery lights rimmed with crepe paper that made a crinkly sound as the breeze hit it. A thousand lights done up in blue and green, and the crowd gathered to both sides behind them, so that the street became an iridescent replica of the Moth, not nearly as wide, but surely as deep and magical.

Around him came the sounds of laughter and polite conversation, each table its own island of charm and anticipation: ladies in white and red dresses that sparkled with sequins when the light caught them, gentlemen in dark blue suits or tuxedos, looking just as ridiculous as Dad had once looked, caught out in the rain.

Dradin ordered a mildly alcoholic drink called a Red Orchid and sipped it as he snuck glances at the couple to his immediate right: a tall, thin man with aquiline features, eyes narrow as papercuts, and rich, gray sideburns, and his consort, a blonde woman in an emerald dress that covered her completely and yet also revealed her completely in the tightness of its fabric. Flushed in the candle light, she laughed too loudly, smiled too quickly, and it made Dradin cringe to watch her make a fool of herself, the man a bigger fool for not putting her at her ease. The man only watched her with a thin smile splayed across his face. Surely when the woman in the window, his love, came to his table, there would be only traces of this awkwardness, this ugliness in the guise of grace?

His love? Glass at his lips, Dradin realized he didn't know her name. It could be Angeline or Melanctha or Galendrace, or even — and his expression darkened as he concentrated *hard*, felt an odd tingling in his temples, finally expelled the name — "Nepenthe," the name of the sweaty woman priest in the jungles. He put down his glass. All this preparation, his nerves on edge, and he didn't even know the name of the woman in the window. A chill went through him, for did he not know her as well as he knew himself?

Soon, the procession made its way down the parade route: the vast, engulfing cloth kites with wire ribs that formed the shapes of giant squid, paper streamers for tentacles running out behind as, lit by their own inner flames, they bumped and spun against the darkened sky. Ships followed them — floats mounted on the rusted hulks of mechanized vehicles, their purpose to re-enact the same scene as the boys with their toy boats: the hunt for the mighty Kraken, the fresh water squid, which made its home in the deepest parts of the Moth, in the place where the river was wide as the sea and twice as mad with silt.

Dradin clapped and said, "Beautiful, beautiful," and, with elegant desperation, ordered another drink, for if he was to be starving and penniless anyway, what was one more expense?

On the parade route, performing wolf hounds followed the floats, then jugglers, mimes, fire eaters, contortionists, and belly dancers. The gangrenous moon began to seep across the sky in dark green hues. The drone of conversations grew more urgent and the cries of the people on the street below, befouled by food, drink, and revelry, became discordant: a fragmented roar of fragmenting desires.

Where was his love? Would she not come? Dradin's head

felt light and hollow, yet heavy as the earth spinning up to greet him, at the possibility. No, it was not a possibility. Dradin ordered yet another Red Orchid.

She would come. Dressed in white and red she would come, around her throat a necklace of intricate blue and green beads, a rough emerald dangling from the center. He would stand to greet her and she would offer her hand to him and he would bow to kiss it. Her skin would be warm to the touch of his lips and his lips would feel warm and electric to her. He would say to her, "Please, take a seat," and pull out her chair. She would acknowledge his chivalry with a slight leftward tip of her head. He would wait for her to sit and then he would sit, wave to a waiter, order her a glass of wine, and then they would talk. Circling in toward how he had first seen her, he would ask her how she liked the book, the necklace. Perhaps both would laugh at the crudity of Dvorak, and at his own shyness, for surely now she could see that he was not truly shy. The hours would pass and with each minute and each witty comment, she would look more deeply into his eyes and he into hers. Their hands would creep forward across the table until, clumsily, she jostled her wine glass and he reached out to keep it from falling — and found her hand instead.

From there, her hand in his, their gaze so intimate across the table, everything would be easy, because it would all be unspoken, but no less eloquent for that. Perhaps they would leave the table, the tavern, traverse the streets in the aftermath of festival. But, no matter what they did, there would be this bond between them: that they had drunk deep of the desire in each other's eyes.

Dradin wiped the sweat from his forehead, took another sip of his drink, looked into the crowd, which more and more merged with the parade, crashing and pushing toward the lights and the performers.

War veterans were marching past: a grotesque assembly of ghost limbs, memories disassembled from the flesh, for not a one had two arms and two legs both. They clattered and shambled forward in their odd company with crutches and wheelchairs and comrades supporting them. They wore the uniforms of a hundred wars and ranged in age from seventeen to seventy; Dradin recognized a few from his hostel. Those who carried sabres waved and twirled their weapons, inciting the crowd, which now pushed and pulled and divided amongst itself like a replicating beast, to shriek and line the parade route ever more closely.

Then, with solemn precision, four men came carrying a coffin, so small as to be for a child, each lending but a single hand to the effort. On occasion, the leader would fling open the top to reveal the empty interior and the crowd would moan and stamp its feet.

Behind the coffin came a caged jungle cat that spat and snarled and worked one enormous pitch paw through bamboo bars. Looking into the dulled but defiant eyes of the cat, Dradin gulped his Red Orchid and thought of the jungle. *The moist heat, the ferns curling into their fetid greenness, the flowers running red, the thick smell of rich black soil on the shovel, the pale gray of the woman's hand, the suddenness of coming upon a savage village, soon to be a ghost place, the savages fled or struck down by disease, the dark eyes and questioning looks on the faces of those he disturbed, bringing his missionary word, the way the forest could be too green, so fraught with scents and tastes and sounds that one could become intoxicated by it, even become feverish within it, drowning in black water, plagued by the curse of no converts.*

Dradin shuddered again from the cold of the drink, and thought he felt the deck beneath him roll and plunge in time to the music of The Ravens. Was it possible that he had never fully recovered from the fever? Was he even now stone-cold mad in the head, or was he simply woozy from Red Orchids? Or could he be, in his final distress, drunk on love? He had precious little else left, a realization accompanied by a not unwelcome thrill of fear. With no job and little money, the only

Dradin, In Love

element of his being he found constant and unyielding, undoubting, was the strength of his love for the woman in the window.

He smiled at the couple at the next table, though no doubt it came out as the sort of drunken leer peculiar to his father. Past relationships had been of an unfortunate nature; he could admit that to himself now. Too platonic, too strange, and always too brief. The jungle did not cotton to long relationships. The jungle ate up long relationships, ground them between its teeth and spat them out. Like the relationship between himself and Nepenthe. Nepenthe. Might the woman in the window also be called Nepenthe? Would she mind if he called her that? Now the deck beneath him really did roll and list like a ship at sea, and he held himself to his chair, pushed the Red Orchid away when he had come once more to rest.

Looking out at the parade, Dradin saw Cadimon Signal and he had to laugh. Cadimon. Good old Cadimon. Was this parade to become like Dvorak's wonderfully ugly tattoo? A trip from past to present? For there indeed was Cadimon, waving to the crowds from a float of gold and white satin, the Living Saint beside him, diplomatically clothed for the occasion in messianic white robes.

"Hah!" Dradin said. "Hah!"

The parade ended with an elderly man leading a live lobster on a leash, a sight that made Dradin laugh until he cried. The lights along the boulevard began to be snuffed out, at first one by one, and then, as the mob descended, ripped out in swathes, so that whole sections were plunged into darkness at once. Beyond them, the great spits no longer turned, abandoned, the meat upon them blackened to ash, and beyond the spits bonfires roared and blazed all the more brightly, as if to make up for the death of the other lights. Now it was impossible to tell parade members from crowd members, so clotted together and at-sea were they, mixed in merriment under the green light of the moon.

Around Dradin, busboys hastily cleaned up tables, helped by barkeepers, and he heard one mutter to another, "It will be bad this year. Very bad. I can feel it." The waiter presented Dradin with the check, tapping his feet while Dradin searched his pockets for the necessary coin, and when it was finally offered, snatching it from his hand and leaving in a flurry of tails and shiny shoes.

Dradin, hollow and tired and sad, looked up at the black-and-green-tinged sky. His love had not come and would not now come, and perhaps had never planned to come, for he only had the word of Dvorak. He did not know how he should feel, for he had never considered this possibility, that he might not meet her. He looked around him — at the table fixtures, the emptying tables, the sudden lull. Now what could he do? He could take a menial job and survive on scraps until he could get a message to his father in Morrow — who then might or might not take pity on him. But for salvation? For redemption?

Fireworks wormholed into the sky and exploded in an umbrella of sparks so that the crowds screamed louder to drown out the noise. Someone jostled him from behind. Wetness dripped down his left shoulder, followed by a curse, and he turned in time to see one of the waiters scurry off with a half-spilled drink.

The smoke from the fireworks descended, mixed with the growing fog come traipsing off the River Moth. It spread more quickly than Dradin would have thought possible, the night smudged with smoke, thick and dark. And who should come out of this haze and into Dradin's gloom but Dvorak, dressed now in green so that the dilute light of the moon passed invisibly over him. His head cocked curiously, like a monkey's, he approached sideways toward Dradin, an appraising look on his face. Was he poisonous like the snake, Dradin thought, or edible, like the insect? Or was he merely a bit of bark to be ignored? For so did Dvorak appraise him. A spark of anger began to smolder in Dradin, for after all Dvorak had made the arrangements and the woman was not here.

"You," Dradin said, raising his voice over the general roar. "You. What're you doing here? You're late...I mean, she's late. She's not coming. Where is she? *Did you lie to me, Dvorak?*"

Dvorak moved to Dradin's side and, with his muscular hands under Dradin's arms, pulled Dradin half way to his feet with such suddenness that he would have fallen over if he hadn't caught himself.

Dradin whirled around, intending to reprimand Dvorak, but found himself speechless as he stared into the dwarf's eyes — dark eyes, so impenetrable, the entire face set like sculpted clay, that he could only stand there and say, weakly, "You said she'd be here."

"Shut up," Dvorak said, and the stiff, coiled menace in the voice caught Dradin between anger and obedience. Dvorak filled the moment with words: "She is here. Nearby. It is Festival night. There is danger everywhere. If she had come earlier, perhaps. But now, now you must meet her elsewhere, in safety. For her safety." Dvorak put a clammy hand on Dradin's arm, but Dradin shook him off.

"Don't touch me. Where's safer than here?"

"Nearby, I tell you. The crowd, the festival. Night is upon us. She will not wait for you."

On the street below, fist fights had broken out. Through the haze, Dradin could hear the slap of flesh on flesh, the snap of bone, the moans of victims. People ran hither and thither, shadows flitting through green darkness.

"Come, sir. *Now.*" Dvorak tugged on Dradin's arm, pulled him close, whispered in Dradin's ear like an echo from another place, another time, the map of his face so inscrutable Dradin could not read it: "You must come *now*. Or not at all. If not at all, you will never see her. She will only see you now. Now! Are you so foolish that you will pass?"

Dradin hesitated, weighing the risks. Where might the dwarf lead him?

Dvorak cursed. "Then do not come. Do not. And take your chances with the Festival."

He turned to leave but Dradin reached down and grabbed his arm.

"Wait," Dradin said. "I will come," and taking a few steps found to his relief that he did not stagger.

"Your love awaits," Dvorak said, unsmiling. "Follow close, sir. You would not wish to become lost from me. It would go hard on you."

"How far — "

"No questions. No talking. Follow."

Dradin sensed the scuffle of feet on pavement behind and in front, and the darkness became claustrophobic, close with the scent of rot and decay

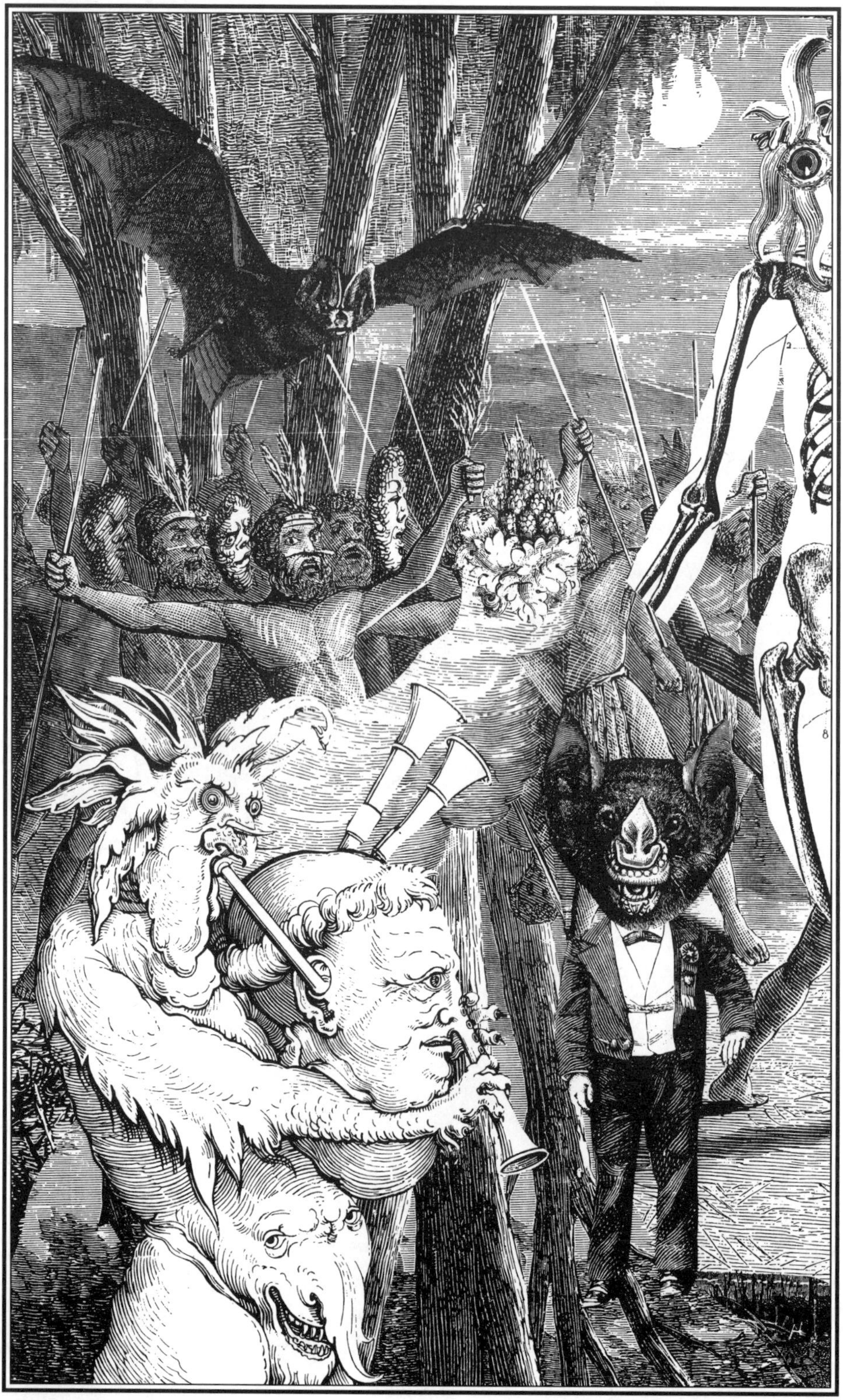

VI.

DVORAK LED DRADIN around the back of *The Drunken Boat* and into an alley, the stones slick with vomit, littered with sharp glass from broken beer and wine bottles, and guarded by a bum muttering an old song from the equinox. Rats waddled on fat legs to eat from half-gnawed drumsticks and soggy buns.

The rats reminded Dradin of the religious quarter and of Cadimon, and then of Cadimon's warning: *"It's not safe for priests to be on the streets after dark during Festival."* He stopped following Dvorak, his head clearer.

"I've changed my mind. I can see her tomorrow at Hoegbotton & Sons."

Dvorak's face clouded like a storm come up from the bottom of the sea as he turned and came back to Dradin. He said, "You have no choice. Follow me."

"No."

"You will never see her then."

"Are you threatening me?"

Dvorak sighed and his overcoat shivered with the blades of a hundred knives. "You will come with me."

"You've already said that."

"Then you will not come?"

"No."

Dvorak punched Dradin in the stomach. The blow felt like an iron ball. All the breath went out of Dradin. The sky spun above him. He doubled over. The side of Dvorak's shoe caught him in the temple, a deep searing pain. Dradin fell heavily on the slick slime and glass of the cobblestones. Glass cut into his palms, his legs, as he twisted and groaned. He tried, groggily, to get to his feet. Dvorak's shoe exploded against his ribs. He screamed, fell onto his side where he lay unmoving, unable to breath except in gasps. Clammy hands put a noose of hemp around his neck, pulled it taut, brought his head up off the ground.

Dvorak held a long, slender blade to Dradin's neck and pulled at the hemp until Dradin was on his knees, looking up into the mottled face. Dradin gasped despite his pain, for it was a different face than only moments before.

Dvorak's features were a sea of conflicting emotions, his mouth twisted to express fear, jealousy, sadness, joy, hatred, as if by encompassing a map of the world he had somehow encompassed all of worldly experience, and that it had driven him mad. In Dvorak's eyes, Dradin saw the dwarf's true detachment from the world and on Dvorak's face he saw the beatific smile of the truly damned, for the face, the flesh, still held the memory of emotion, even if the mind behind the flesh had forgotten.

"In the name of God, Dvorak," Dradin said.

Dvorak's mouth opened and the tongue clacked down and the voice came, distant and thin as memory, "You are coming with me, sir. On your feet."

Dvorak pulled savagely on the rope. Dradin gurgled and forced his fingers between the rope and his neck.

"On your feet, I said."

Dradin groaned and rolled over. "I can't."

Dradin, In Love

The knife jabbed into the back of his neck. "Soft! Get up, or I'll kill you here."

Dradin forced himself up, though his head was woozy and his stomach felt punctured beyond repair. He avoided looking down into Dvorak's eyes. To look would only confirm that he was dealing with a monster.

"I am a priest."

"I know you are a priest," Dvorak said.

"Your soul will burn in Hell," Dradin said.

A burst of laughter. "I was born there, sir. My face reflects its flames. Now, you will walk ahead of me. You will not run. You will not raise your voice. If you do, I shall choke you and gut you where you stand."

"I have money," Dradin said heavily, still trying to let air into his lungs. "I have gold."

"And we will take it. Walk! There is not much time."

"Where are we going?"

"You will know when we get there."

When Dradin still did not move, Dvorak shoved him forward. Dradin began to walk, Dvorak so close behind he imagined he could feel the point of the blade against the small of his back.

THE GREEN LIGHT of the moon stained everything except the bonfires the color of toads and dead grass. The bonfires called with their siren song of flame until crowds gathered at each one to dance, shout, and fight. Dradin soon saw that Dvorak's route — through alley after alley, over barricades — was intended to avoid the bonfires. There was now no cool wind in all the city, for around every corner they turned, the harsh rasp of the bonfires met them. To all sides, buildings sprang up out of the fog — dark, silent, menacing.

As they crossed a bridge, over murky water thick with sewage and the flotsam of the festivities, a man hobbled toward them. His left ear had been severed from his head. He cradled part of someone's leg in his arms. He moaned and when he saw Dradin, Dvorak masked by shadow, he shouted, "Stop them! Stop them!" only to continue on into the darkness, and Dradin helpless anyway. Soon after, following the trail of blood, a hooting mob of ten or twelve youths came a-hunting, tawny-limbed and fresh for the kill. They yelled catcalls and taunted Dradin, but when they saw that he was a prisoner they turned their attentions back to their own prey.

The buildings became black shadows tinged green, the street underfoot rough and ill-hewn. A wall stood to either side.

A deep sliver of fear pulled Dradin's nerves taut. "How much further?" he asked.

"Not far. Not far at all."

The mist deepened until Dradin could not tell the difference between the world with his eyes shut and the world with his eyes open. Dradin sensed the scuffle of feet on the pavement behind and in front, and the darkness became claustrophobic, close with the scent of rot and decay.

"We are being followed," Dradin said.

"You are mistaken."

"I hear them!"

"Shut up! It's not far. Trust me."

"Trust me?" Did Dvorak realize the irony of those words? How foolish that they should converse at all, the knife at his back and the hushed breathing from behind and ahead, stalking them. Fear raised the hairs along his arms and heightened his senses, distorting and magnifying every sound.

Their journey ended where the trees were less thick and the fog had been swept aside. Walls did indeed cordon them in, gray walls that ended abruptly ten feet ahead in a welter of shadows that rustled and quivered like dead leaves lifted by the wind, but there was no wind.

Dradin's temples pounded and his breath caught in his throat. On another street, parallel but out of sight, a clock doled out the hours, one through eleven, and revellers tooted on horns or screamed out names or called to the moon in weeping, distant, fading voices.

Dvorak shoved Dradin forward until they came to an open gate, ornately filigreed, and beyond the gate, through the bars, the brooding headstones of a vast graveyard. Mausoleums and memorials, single tombs and groups, families dead together under the thick humus, the young and the old alike feeding the worms, feeding the earth.

The graveyard was overgrown with grass and weeds so that the headstones swam in a sea of green. Beyond these fading statements of life after death writ upon the fissured stones, riven and made secretive by the moonlight, lay the broken husks of trains, haphazard and strewn across the landscape. The twisted metal of engines, freight cars, and cabooses gleamed darkly green and the patina of broken glass windows, held together by moss, shone especially bright, like vast, reflective eyes. Eyes that still held a glimmer of the past when coal had coursed through their engines like blood and brimstone, and their compartments had been busy with the footsteps of those same people who now lay beneath the earth.

The industrial district. Dradin was in the industrial district and now he knew that due south was his hostel and southwest was Hoegbotton & Sons and the River Moth beyond it.

"I do not see her," Dradin said, to avoid looking ahead to the squirming shadows.

Dvorak's face as the dwarf turned to him was a sickly green and his mouth a cruel slit of darkness. "Should you see her, do you think? I am leading you to a graveyard, missionary. Pray, if you wish."

At those words, Dradin would have run, would have taken off into the mist, not caring if Dvorak found him and gutted him, such was his terror. But then the creeping tread of the creatures resolved itself. The sound grew louder, coming up behind and ahead of him. As he watched, the shadows became shapes and then figures, until he could see the glinty eyes and glinty knives of a legion of silent, waiting mushroom dwellers. Behind them, hopping and rustling, came toads and rats, their eyes bright with darkness. The sky thickened with the swooping shapes of bats.

"Surely," Dradin said, "surely there has been a mistake."

In a sad voice, his face strangely mournful and moonlike, Dvorak said, "There have indeed been mistakes, but they are yours. Take off your clothes."

Dradin backed away, into the arms of the leathery, stretched, musty folk behind. Cringing from their touch, he leapt forward.

"I have money," Dradin said to Dvorak. "I will give you money. My father has money."

Dvorak's smile turned sadly sweeter and sweetly sadder. "How you waste words when you have so few words left to waste. Remove your clothes or they will do it for you," and he motioned to the mushroom dwellers. A hiss of menace rose from their assembled ranks as they pressed closer, closer still, until he could not escape the dry, piercing rot of them, nor the sound of their shambling gait.

He took off his shoes, his socks, his trousers, his shirt, his underwear, folding each item carefully, until his pale body gleamed and he saw himself in his mind's eye as switching positions with the Living Saint. How he would have loved to see the hoary ejaculator now, coming to his rescue, but there was no hope of that. Despite the chill, Dradin held his hands over his penis rather than his chest. What did modesty matter, and yet still he did it.

Dvorak hunched nearer, hand taut on the rope, and used his knife to pull the clothes over to him. He went through the pockets, took the remaining coins, and then put the clothes over his shoulder.

"Please, let me go," Dradin said. "I beg you." There was a tremor in his voice but, he marveled, only a tremor, only a hint of fear.

Who would have guessed that so close to his own murder he could be so calm?

"I cannot let you go. You no longer belong to me. You are a priest, are you not? They pay well for the blood of priests."

"My friends will come for me."

"You have no friends in this city."

"Where is the woman from the window?"

Dvorak smiled with a smugness that turned Dradin's stomach. A spark of anger spread all up and down his back and made his teeth grind together. The graveyard gate was open. He had run through graveyards once, with Anthony — graveyards redolent with the stink of old metal and ancient technologies — but was that not where they wished him to go?

"In the name of God, what have you done with her?"

"You are too clever by half," Dvorak said. "She is still in Hoegbotton & Sons."

"At this hour?"

"Yes."

"W-w-why is she there?" His fear for her, deeper into him than his own anger, made his voice quiver.

Dvorak's mask cracked. He giggled and cackled and stomped his foot. "Because, because, sir, sir, I have taken her to pieces. I have dismembered her!" And from behind and in front and all around, the horrible, galumphing, harumphing laughter of the mushroom dwellers.

Dismembered her.

The laughter, mocking and cruel, set him free from his inertia. Clear and cold he was now, made of ice, always keeping the face of his beloved before him. He could not die until he had seen her body.

Dradin yanked on the rope and, as Dvorak fell forward, wrenched free the noose. He kicked the dwarf in the head and heard a satisfying howl of pain, but did not wait, did not watch — he was already running through the gate before the mushroom dwellers could stop him. His legs felt like cold metal, like the churning pistons of the old coal-chewing trains. He ran as he had never run in all his life, even with Tony. He ran like a man possessed, recklessly dodging tombstones and high grass, while behind came the angry screams of Dvorak, the slithery swiftness of the mushroom dwellers. And still Dradin laughed as he went — bellowing as he jumped atop a catacomb of mausoleums and leapt between monuments, trapped for an instant by abutting tombstones, and then up and running again, across the top of yet another broad sepulchre. He found his voice and shouted to his pursuers, "Catch me! Catch me!", and cackled his own mad cackle, for he was as naked as the day he had entered the world and his beloved was dead and he had nothing left in the world to lose. Lost as he might be, lost as he might always be, yet the feeling of freedom was heady. It made him giddy and drunk with his own power. He crowed to his pursuers, he needled them, only to pop up elsewhere, thrilling to the hardness of his muscles, the toughness gained in the jungle where all else had been lost.

Finally, he came to the line of old trains, byzantine and convoluted and dark, surrounded by the smell of dank, rusting metal. One backward glance before entering the maze revealed that the mushroom dwellers, led by Dvorak, had reached the last line of tombstones, fifty feet away.

— but a glance only before he swung himself into the side door of an engine, walked on the balls of his feet into the cool darkness. Hushed quiet. This was what he needed now. Quiet and stealth in equal measures so that he could reach the relative safety of the street beyond the trains. His senses heightened, he could hear *them* coming, the whispers between them as they spread out to search the compartments.

Spider-like, Dradin moved as he heard them move, shadowing them but out of sight — into their clutches and out again with a finesse he had not known he possessed — always working his way farther into the jungle of metal. Train tracks. Dining cars. Engines split open by the years, so that he hid

Dradin, In Love

among their most secret parts and came out again when danger had passed him by, a pale figure flecked with rust.

Ahead, when he dared to take his gaze from his pursuers, Dradin could see the uniform darkness of the wall and, from beyond, the red flashes of a bonfire. Two rows of cars lay between him and the wall. He crept forward through the gaping doorway of a dining car —

— just as, cloaked by shadow, Dvorak entered the car from the opposite end. Dradin considered backing out of the car, but no: Dvorak would hear him. Instead, he crouched down, hidden from view by an overturned table, a salt-and-pepper shaker still nailed to it.

Dvorak's footsteps came closer, accompanied by raspy breathing and the shivery threat of the knives beneath his coat. A single shout from Dvorak and the mushroom dwellers would find him.

Dvorak stopped in front of the overturned table. Dradin could smell him now, the *must* of mushroom dweller, the *tang* of Moth silt. The breathing.

Dradin sprang up and slapped his left hand across Dvorak's mouth, spun him around as he grunted, and grappled for Dvorak's knife. Dvorak opened his mouth to bite Dradin. Dradin stuck his fist in Dvorak's mouth, muffling his own scream as the teeth bit down. Now Dvorak could make no sound and the dwarf frantically tried to expel Dradin's fist. Dradin did not let him. The knife seesawed from Dvorak's side up to Dradin's clavicle and back again. Dvorak thrashed about, trying to dislodge Dradin's hold on him, trying to face his enemy. Dradin, muscles straining, entangled Dvorak's legs in his and managed to keep him in the center of the compartment. If they banged up against the sides it would be as loud as a word from Dvorak's mouth. But the knife was coming too close to Dradin's throat. He smashed Dvorak's hand against a railing, a sound that sent up an echo Dradin thought the mushroom dwellers must surely hear. No one came as the knife fell from Dvorak's hand. Dvorak tried to grasp inside his jacket for another. Dradin pulled a knife from within the jacket first. As Dvorak withdrew his own weapon, Dradin's blade was already buried deep in his throat.

Dradin felt the dwarf's body go taut and then lose its rigidity, while the mouth came loose of his fist and a thick, viscous liquid dribbled down his knife arm.

Dradin turned to catch the body as it fell, so that as he held it and lowered it to the ground, his hand throbbing and bloody, he could see Dvorak's eyes as the life left them. The tattoo, in that light, became all undone, the red dots of cities like wounds, sliding off to become merely a crisscross of lines. Dark blood coated the front of his shirt.

Dradin mumbled a prayer under his breath from reflex alone, for some part of him — the part of him that had laughed to watch the followers of St. Solon placing sparrows in coffins — insisted that death was unremarkable, undistinguished, and, ultimately, unimportant, for it happened every day, everywhere. Unlike the jungle, Nepenthe's severed hand, here there was no amnesia, no fugue. There was only the body beneath him and an echo in his ears, the memory of his mother's voice as she *thrulled* from deep in her throat a death march, a funeral veil stitched of words and music. How could he feel hatred? He could not. He felt only emptiness.

He heard, with newly preternatural senses, the movement of mushroom dwellers nearby, and resting Dvorak's head against the cold metal floor, left the compartment, a shadow against the deeper shadow of the wrecked and rotted wheels.

Now it was easy for Dradin, slipping between tracks, huddling in dining compartments, the mushroom dwellers blind to his actions. The two rows of cars between him and the wall became one row and then he was at the wall. He climbed it tortuously, the rough stone cutting into his hands and feet. When he reached the top, he swung up and over to the other side.

Dradin, In Love

AH, THE BOULEVARD beyond, for now Dradin wondered if he should return to the graveyard and hide there. Strewn across the boulevard were scaffolds and from the scaffolds men and women had been hung so that they lolled and, limp, had the semblance of rag dolls. Rag dolls in tatters, the flesh pulled from hindquarters, groins, chests, the red meeting the green of the moon and turning black. Eyes stared sightless. The harsh wind carried the smell of offal. Dogs bit at the feet, the legs, the bodies so thick that as Dradin walked forward, keen for the sound of mushroom dwellers behind him, he had to push aside and duck under the limbs of the dead. Blood splashed his shoulders and he breathed in gasps and held his side, as if something pained him, though it was only the sight of the bodies that pained him. When he realized that he still wore a noose of his own, he pulled it over his head with such speed that it cut him and left a burn.

Past the hanging bodies and burning buildings and flamed out motored vehicles, only to see . . . stilt men carrying severed heads, which they threw to the waiting crowds, who kicked and tossed them . . . a man disemboweled, his intestines streaming out into the gutter as his attackers continued to hack him apart and he clutched at their legs . . . a woman assaulted against a brick wall by ten men who held her down as they cut and raped her . . . fountains full of floating, bloated bodies, the waters turned red-black with blood . . . glimpses of the bonfires, bodies stacked for burning in the dozens . . . a man and woman decapitated, still caught in an embrace, on their knees in the murk of rising mist . . . the unearthly screams, the taste of blood rising in the air, the smell of fire and burning flesh . . . and the female riders on their wooden horses, riding over the bodies of the dead, splashing in the blood, their eyes still turned inward, that they might not know the horrors of the night.

Oh, that he could rip his own eyes from his sockets! He did not wish to see and yet could not help but see if he wished to live. In the face of such carnage his killing of Dvorak became the gentlest of mercies. Bile rose in his throat and, sick with grief and horror, he vomited beside an abandoned horse buggy. When the sickness had passed, he gathered his wits, found a landmark he recognized, and by passing through lesser alleys and climbing over the rooftops of one-story houses set close together, came once again to his hostel.

The hostel was empty and silent, and Dradin crept, limping from glass in his foot and the ache in his muscles, up to the second floor and his room. Once inside, he did not even try to wash off the blood, the dirt, the filth, did not put on clothes, but stumbled to his belongings and stuffed his pictures, *The Refraction of Light in a Prison*, and his certificate from the religious college into the knapsack. He stood in the center of the room, knapsack over his left shoulder, the machete held in his right hand, breathing heavily, trying to remember who he might be and where he might be and what he should do now. He shuffled over to the window and looked down on the valley. What he saw made him laugh, a high-pitched sound so repugnant to him that he closed his mouth immediately.

The valley lay under a darkness pricked by soft, warm lights. No bonfires raged in the valley below. No one hung from scaffolding, tongues blue and purpling. No one bathed in the blood of the dead.

Seeing the valley so calm, Dradin remembered when he had wondered if, perhaps, his beloved lived there, amid the peace where there were no missionaries. No Living Saints. No Cadimons. No Dvoraks. He looked toward the door. It was a perilous door, a deceitful door, for the world lay beyond it in all its brutality. He stood there for several beats of his heart, thinking of how beautiful the woman had looked in the third story window, how he had thrilled to see her there. What a beautiful place the world had been then, so long ago.

Machete held ready, Dradin walked to the door and out into the night.

It seemed to Dradin as he looked at the woman sitting in the chair that he had not seen her in a hundred, a thousand, years, that he saw her now across some great becalmed ocean or desert

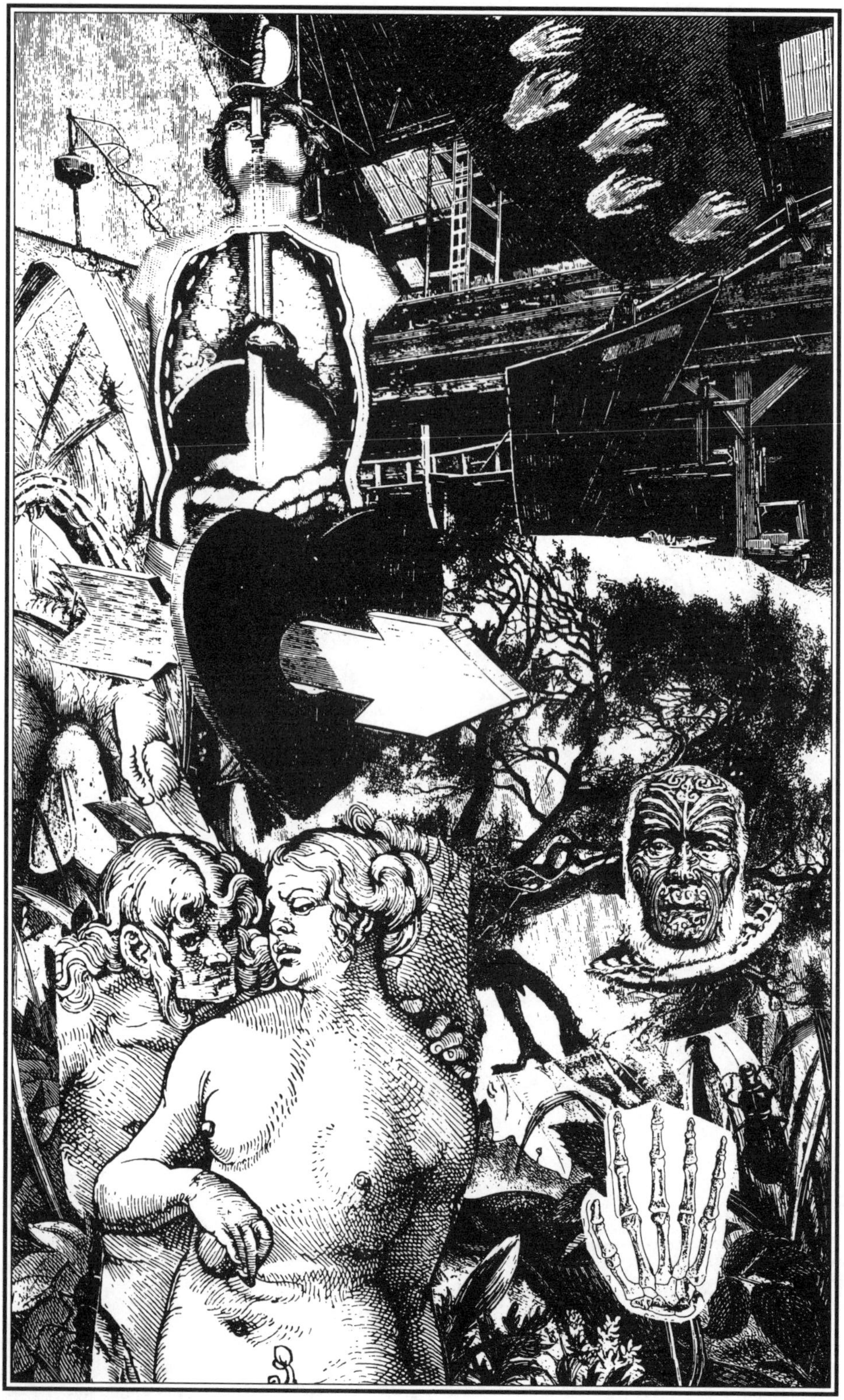

VII.

WHEN DRADIN HAD at last fought his way back to Hoegbotton & Sons, Albumuth Boulevard was deserted except for a girl in a ragged flower print dress. She listened to a tattered phonograph that played Voss Bender tunes.

> *In the deep of winter:*
> *Snatches of song*
> *Through the branches*
> *Brittle as bone.*
>
> *You'll not see my face*
> *But there I'll be,*
> *Frost in my hair,*
> *My hunger hollowing me.*

The sky had cleared and the cold, white pricks of stars shone through the black of night, the green-tinge of moon. The black in which moon and stars floated was absolute; it ate the light of the city, muted everything but the shadows, which multiplied and rippled outward. Behind Dradin, sounds of destruction grew nearer, but here the stores were ghostly but whole. And yet here too men, women, and children hung from the lamp posts and looked down with lost, vacant, and wondering stares.

The girl sat on her knees in front of the phonograph. Over her lay the shadow of the great lambent eye, shiny and saucepan blind, of one of the colorful cloth squid, its tentacles rippling in the breeze. Bodies were caught in its *faux* coils, sprawled and sitting upright in the maw and craw of the beast, as if they had drowned amid the tentacles, washed ashore still entangled and stiffening.

Dradin walked up to the girl. She had brown hair and dark, unreadable eyes with long lashes. She was crying, although her face had long ago been wiped clean of sorrow and of joy. She watched the phonograph as if it were the last thing in the world that made sense to her.

He nudged her. "Go. Go on! Get off the street. You're not safe here."

She did not move, and he looked at her with a mixture of sadness and exasperation. There was nothing he could do. Events were flowing away from him, caught in the undertow of a river stronger than the Moth. It was all he could do to preserve his own life, his bloody machete proof of the dangers of the bureaucratic district by which he had come again to Albumuth. The same languid, nostalgic streets of daylight had become killing grounds, a thousand steely-eyed murderers hiding amongst the vetch and honeysuckle. It was there that he had rediscovered the white-faced mimes, entangled in the ivy, features still in death.

Dradin walked past the girl until Hoegbotton & Sons lay before him. The dull red brick seemed brighter in the night, as if it reflected the fires burning throughout the city.

And so it ends where it began, Dradin thought. In front of the very same Hoegbotton & Sons building. Were he not such a coward, he should have ended it there much sooner.

Dradin, In Love

Dradin stole up the stairs to the door. He smashed the glass of the door with his already mangled fist, grunting with pain. The pain pulsed far away, disconnected from him in his splendid nakedness. *Pinpricks on the souls of distant sinners.* Dradin swung the door open and shut it with such a clatter that he was sure someone had heard him and would come loping down the boulevard after him. But no one came and his feet, naked and dirty and cut, continued to slap the steps inside so loudly that surely she would run away if she was still alive, thinking him an intruder. But where to run? He could hear his own labored breathing as he navigated the stairs: the sound filled the landing; it filled the spaces between the steps; and it filled him with determination, for it was the most vital sign that he still lived, despite every misfortune.

Dradin laughed, but it came out ragged around the edges. His mind sagged under the weight of carnage: the cries of looting, begging; the sound of men swinging by their necks or their testicles or their feet. Swinging all across a city grown suddenly wise and quiet in their deaths.

But that was out there, in the city. In here, Dradin promised, he would not lose himself to such images. He would not lose the threads.

CURIOUS, BUT ON reaching the door to the third floor, Dradin paused, halted, did not yet grasp the iron knob. For this door led to the window. He had engraved her position so perfectly on the interstices of his memory that he knew exactly where she must be . . . One moment more of hesitation, and then Dradin entered her.

A room. Darkened. The smell of sawdust packing and boxes. Not the right room. Not her room. The antechamber only, for receiving visitors, perhaps, the walls lined with decadent objects d' arte, and beyond that, an open doorway, leading to . . .

The next room was lined with Occidental shadow puppets that looked like black scars, seared and shaped into human forms: bodies entwined in lust and devout in prayer, bodies engaged in murder and in business. Harlequins and pierrotts with bashful red eyes and sharp teeth lay on their backs, feet up in the air. Jungle plants trellised and cat's cradled the interior, freed from terrariums, while a clutter of other things hidden by the shadows beckoned him with their strange, angular shapes. The smell of moist rot mixed with the stench of mushroom dweller and the sweet bitter of sweat, as if the very walls labored for the creation of such wonderful monstrosities.

She still faced the window, but set back from it, in a wooden chair, so that the curling curious fires ravaging the city beyond could not sear her face. The light from these fires created a zone of blackness and Dradin could see only her black hair draped across the chair back.

It seemed to Dradin as he looked at the woman sitting in the chair that he had not seen her in a hundred, a thousand, years; that he saw her across some great becalmed ocean or desert, she only a shape like the shadow puppets. He moved closer.

His woman, the woman of his dreams, gazed off into the charred red-black air, the opposite street, or even toward the hidden River Moth beyond. He thought he saw a hint of movement as he approached her — a slight uplifting of one arm — she no longer concerned with the short view, but with the long view, the perspective that nothing of the moment mattered or would ever matter. It had been Dvorak's view, with the map that had taken over his body. It was Cadimon's view, not allowing the priest to take pity on a former student.

"My love," Dradin said, and again, "My love," as he walked around so he could see the profile of her face. A white sheet covered her body, but her face, oh, her face . . . her eyebrows were thin and dark, her eyes like twin blue flames, her nose small, unobtrusive, her skin white, white, white, but with a touch of color that drew him down to the sumptuous curve of her mouth, the bead of sweat upon the upper lip, the fine hairs placed to seduce, to trick; the way in which the clothes clung to her body and made it seem to curve, the arms placed upon the arms of the chair, so naturally that there was no artifice in having done so. Might she . . . could she . . . still be . . . alive?

Dradin pulled aside the white sheet — and screamed, for there lay the torso, the legs severed and in pieces beneath, but placed cleverly for the illusion of life, the head balanced atop the torso, dripping neither blood nor precious humors, but as dry and slick and perfect as if it had never known a body. Which it had not. From head to toe, Dradin's beloved was a mannequin, an artifice, a deception. *Hoegbotton & Sons, specialists in all manner of profane and Occidental technologies . . .*

Dradin's mouth opened and closed but no sound came from him. Now he could see the glassy finish of her features, the innate breakability of a creature made of papier-mache and metal and porcelain and clay, mixed and beaten and blown and sandpapered and engraved and made up like any other woman. A testimony to the clockmaker's craft, for at the hinges and joints of the creature dangled broken filaments and wires and gimshaw circuitry. Fool. He was thrice a fool.

Dradin circled the woman, his body shivering, his hands reaching out to caress the curve of cheekbone, only to pull back before he touched skin. The jungle fever beat within him, fell away in *decrescendo*, then again *crescendo*. Twice more around and his arm darted out against his will and he touched her cheek. Cold. So cold. So monstrously cold against the warmth of his body. Cold and dead in her beauty despite the heat and the bonfires roaring outside. Dead. Not alive. Never alive.

As he touched her, as he saw all of her severed parts and how they fit together, something small and essential broke inside him; broke so he couldn't ever fix it. Now he saw Nepenthe in his mind's eye in all of her darkness and grace. Now he could see her as a person, not an idea. Now he could see her nakedness, remember the way she had felt under him — smooth and moist and warm — never moving as he made love to her.

As he took her though she did not want to be taken. If ever he had lost his faith it was then, as he lost himself in the arms of a woman indifferent to him, indifferent to the world. He saw again the flash of small hand, severed and gray, and saw again his own hand, holding the blade. Her severed hand. His hand holding the blade. Coming to in the burning missionary station, severed of his memory, severed from his faith, severed from his senses by the fever. Her severed gray hand in his and in the other the machete.

Dradin dropped the machete and it landed with a clang next to the mannequin's feet.

Feverish, he had crawled back from his jungle expedition, the sole survivor, only to find that the people he had gone out to convert had come to the station and burned it to the ground . . . fallen unconscious, and come to with the hand in his, Nepenthe naked and dead next to him. Betrayal.

The shattered pieces within came loose in an exhalation of breath. He could not contain himself any longer, and he sobbed there, at the mannequin's feet, and as he hugged her to him, the fragile balance came undone and her body scattered into pieces all around him, the head staring up at him from the floor.

"I killed her I did I killed her I didn't kill her I didn't mean to I meant to I didn't mean to she made me I let her I wanted her I couldn't have her I never wanted her I wanted her not the way I wanted I couldn't I meant to I couldn't have meant to but I did it I don't know if I did it — *I can't remember!*"

Dradin slid to the floor and lay there for a long while, exhausted, gasping for breath, his mouth tight, his jaw unfamiliar to him. He welcomed the pain from the splinters that cut into his flesh from the floorboards. He felt hollow inside, indifferent, so fatigued, so despairing that he did not know if he could ever regain his feet.

But, after a time, Dradin looked full into the woman's eyes and a grim smile spread across his face. He thought he could hear his mother's voice mixed with the sound of rain thrumming across a roof. He thought he could hear his father reading the adventures of Juliette and Justine to him. He knelt beside the head and caressed its cheek. He lay beside the head and admired its features.

He heard himself say it.

"I love you."

He still loved her. He could not deny it. Could not. It was a love that might last a minute or a day, an hour or a month, but for the moment, in his need, it seemed as permanent as the moon and the stars, and as cold.

It did not matter that she was in pieces, that she was not real, for he could see now that she was his salvation. Had he not been in love with what he saw in the third story window, and had what he had seen through that window changed in its essential nature? Wasn't she better suited to him than if she had been real, with all the avarices and hungers and needs and awkwardnesses that create disappointment? He had invented an entire history for this woman and now his expectations of her would never change and she would never age, never criticize him, never tell him he was too fat or too sloppy or too neat, and he would never have to raise his voice to her.

It struck Dradin as he basked in the glow of such feelings, as he watched the porcelain lines of the head while shouts grew louder and the gallows jerked and swung merrily all across the city. It struck him that he could not betray this woman. There would be no decaying, severed hand. No flowers sprayed red with blood. No crucial misunderstandings. The thought blossomed bright and blinding in his head. He could not betray her. Even if he set her head upon the mantel and took a lover there, in front of her, as his father might once have done to his mother, those eyes would not register the sin. This seemed to him, in that moment, to be a form of wisdom beyond even Cadimon, a wisdom akin to the vision that had struck him as he stood in the backyard of the old house in Morrow.

Dradin embraced the pieces of his lover, luxuriating in the smooth and shiny feel of her, the precision of her skin. He rose to a knee, cradling his beloved's head in his shaking arms. Was he moaning now? Was he screaming now? Who could tell?

With careful deliberateness, Dradin took his lover's head and walked into the antechamber, and then out the door. The third floor landing was dark and quiet. He began to walk down the stairs, descending slowly at first, taking pains to slap his feet against each step. But when he reached the second floor landing, he became more frantic, as if to escape what lay behind him, until by the time he reached the first floor and burst out from the shattered front door, he was running hard, knapsack bobbing against his back.

Down the boulevard, seen through the folds of the squid float, a mob approached, holding candles and torches and lanterns. Stores flared and burned behind them . . .

Dradin spared them not a glance, but continued to run — past the girl and her phonograph, still playing Voss Bender, and past *Borges Bookstore*, in the shadow of which prowled the black panther from the parade, and then beyond, into the unknown. Sidestepping mushroom dwellers at their dark harvest, their hands full of mushrooms from which spores broke off like dandelion tufts, and the last of the revelers of the Festival of the Freshwater Squid, their trajectories those of pendulums and their tongues blue if not black, arms slack at their sides. Through viscera and the limbs of babies stacked in neat piles. Amongst the heehaws and gimgobs, the drunken dead and the lolly lashers with their dark whips. Weeping now, tears without end. Mumbling and whispering endearments to his beloved, running strong under the mad, mad light of the moon — headed forever and always for the docks and the muscular waters of the River Moth, which would take him and his lover as far as he might wish, though perhaps not far enough.

ACKNOWLEDGMENTS

The author would like to thank Dale Bailey, Nathan Ballingrud, Duane Bray, Cliff Burns, Jeff Martel, Penelope Miller, Luke O'Grady, Mike Olson, Wade Tarzia, and Bruce Taylor for their close reading of "Dradin, In Love" in its various incarnations. Thanks also to the Golden Prince, Robyn Hitchcock: the lyrics on page 67 were inspired by his song "City of Shame" from his album Black Snake, Diamond Role. Finally, the author would like to dedicate this book to the late Angela Stalker.

ABOUT THE AUTHOR

Jeff VanderMeer's surreal short fiction has appeared in over 120 magazines and anthologies in six languages in 12 countries. A collection of his short fiction, The Book of Lost Places, will be published in August 1996 by Dark Regions Press as part of their Selected Works series. Recently, he won a 1994 Rhysling Award for poetry and a 1995-1996 $5,000 Florida Individual Artist Fellowship for fiction. He also co-edits a fiction anthology entitled Leviathan. Two novels, "Mapping the Beast" and "The Refraction of Light in a Prison," are currently underway. Research for Dradin, In Love included stints as a grave digger, a cutlery salesman, a mushroom picker, an assistant to a retired Italian opera singer, and buyer for a well-known import-export business. VanderMeer lives in Florida, where he enjoys reading, racquetball, and long, protracted arguments with virtual strangers.

ABOUT THE ARTIST

Michael Shores has been an active artist and musician since 1977. He was a member of the influential Punkt/Data Gallery from 1977 to 1979. This art collective was also responsible for Skunk Piss Magazine, one of the pioneer publications utilizing a free editorial format. After a violent accident which nearly cost him his life, he withdrew from the art world to pursue music. In 1981, he met his future wife, Angela Mark, with whom he has collaborated with since. During the 1980s, Shores and Mark continued musical activities as well as founding 88 ROOM Art Gallery with Andrew Guthrie. They now publish their own work as well as other artists and poets under American Living Press. Shores' collage illustrations have been featured in numerous publications. For more information on his work, please write to: American Living Press, P.O. Box 901, Allston, MA 02134.

THE TYPOGRAPHY

The typeface chosen for the body text of this book is 12 pt. Garamond, a common but elegant and readable font developed in France in the 1700s.

Book Antiqua is, of course, used by Borges Bookstore for all of its signs, such as the one on page 7 (reprinted by kind permission of Borges Bookstore), and for its other promotional materials.

The excerpt from "The Refraction of Light in a Prison" reproduced on page 32 is printed in Bookman Old Style, a rarity for that mystical text, since most of the chapters are set in a derivative of Baskerville.